the Lie

the Lie

A NOVEL

Fredrica Wagman

ZOLAND BOOKS
AN IMPRINT OF STEERFORTH PRESS
HANOVER, NEW HAMPSHIRE

For information about permission to reproduce
selections from this book, write to:
Steerforth Press L.L.C., 45 Lyme Road, Suite 208,
Hanover, New Hampshire 03755

Library of Congress Cataloging-in-Publication Data
Wagman, Fredrica.
 The lie : a novel / Fredrica Wagman. — 1st ed.
    p. cm.
 ISBN 978-1-58642-157-1
1. Young women — Fiction. 2. Hayworth, Rita, 1918-1987 — Influence
— Fiction. 3. Sexual abuse victims — Fiction. 4. Psychological fiction.
5. Domestic fiction. I. Title.
 PS3573.A36L54 2009
 813'.54—dc22
            2008044689

This novel is a work of fiction. Names, characters, places, and incidents are
either the products of the author's imagination or are used fictitiously. Any
resemblance to actual persons, living or dead, events, or locales is entirely
coincidental.

FIRST EDITION

for
L.S.

Errors are the heart of life
PHILIP ROTH

part one

then

one

I met him in the park one week to the day after my father died. There he was, an average-looking fellow, nothing special, wearing a yellow sport shirt with one of those little alligators above the pocket, khaki pants, and dark horn-rimmed glasses — completely average until you saw his fingers.

If you saw him sitting on the bus or walking down the street chances are you'd never notice him, not for a second, just another leaf on the tree you'd think . . . unless you caught a glimpse of his thick, childlike hands — his fat peasant hands that were almost like primitive art — each shocking finger round and wide at the base, but instead of it getting slightly narrower as it progressed like most fingers do, it kept all its fat round wideness all the way up to the nail where there was a certain unusual thickening . . . a rather bulbous thickening you might say all around the nail head itself, so that each finger looked exactly like a penis . . . and there were ten of them . . . ten perfect penis fingers . . . I couldn't take my eyes away.

Otherwise, he was on the swarthy side . . . dark and skinny with something gangster, some quality about him like those mobsters you see on the evening news being hauled off after murdering someone or blowing up a bank, only this fellow had nothing dangerous, you could tell that this was no gangster in his neatly tucked-in shirt, his expensive brown leather belt, and dark horn-rimmed glasses, but rather, here was someone tired — weary . . . someone with something all chewed-up about him like he belonged to that secret society I once read about called The Sad Men, which for some reason made him extremely appealing as he sat down beside me, smiled, and offered me a cigarette.

His name he said was Solomon Columbus, which I frankly thought was an awful name and probably he did too because he said to just call him Columbus as he pointed to the old Belgravia Hotel across the park, which he said was where he lived.

Then something about what he did as he handed me his card — a family business he said — something about chickens and eggs in partners with an aunt and uncle in Atlantic City, but I wasn't listening . . . I didn't catch much of it because his fingers were so shocking — so blatant — so flagrant and outrageous that it was almost embarrassing to look at them . . . and yet I couldn't take my eyes away . . . I wanted to touch them, grab them, hold them, put my hand around each one and squeeze.

It was on one of those scorching August afternoons when all the leaves on the ground were curled and crisp from so much heat, the city a desert by then of blazing concrete with the blistering glare of the sun smearing the whole airless afternoon; it hadn't rained for so long that it finally felt like it might never rain again as we sat on the bench staring at each other as we were smoking our cigarettes.

two

Talking began like a train slowly chugging out . . . the halting, self-conscious awkward embarrassment of trying to start something up because eventually you have to say something . . . you can't just sit there . . . somehow or other you have to throw out a stake and hope it takes . . . somewhere . . . somehow . . . and worse, it was I who had to get things rolling because it was he who sat down beside me and smiled as he offered me the cigarette, so now it was up to me — my turn.

They say that as you're dying you see your whole life flashing past down to the most minute detail, and I would say that if that's true, which I doubt, having seen people die and noticing that nothing flashes past, they just want to live another minute — but if it's true, I'll remember the hideousness of ever having to utter my name out loud to any living soul because I've always felt that names are too private — too personal, maybe the most intimately revealing thing a person has, which the sad gloomy fellow sitting next to me with the astonishing penis fingers seemed to sense because he was kind enough to offer me another cigarette . . . as I began to slowly . . . torturously . . . eke out that dead giveaway, all right . . . now I was caught . . . now he had me . . . because names tell it all . . . the trick was not to die of shame as I looked down, not daring to meet his eyes as

I murmured that my name was Ramona Smollens but deep within me on the very most inside place I said it was Rhonda Smollens, whom I sometimes called Rita Smollens in honor of Rita Hayworth, who from the time I was very little I idolized with my whole soul I told him as I looked straight at him for a moment, daring to hope that maybe he'd understand that because of Rita Hayworth I sometimes lost sight of everything . . . schoolwork, friends, parties . . . so mesmerized was I by this exquisite creature, this most splendid masterpiece of pure perfection as I'd gaze spellbound at her as I'd sit in the back of the Egyptian Movie Theater watching wonderstruck on Saturday afternoons — her red hair flying as her thick black heels were bang bang banging banging banging as she was snapping her castanets above her head . . . this flawless majestic wondrous being with the most gorgeous hands I had ever seen.

And then out of nowhere, like a bolt of lightning streaking out of my mouth — suddenly I blurted out to this complete stranger that a week ago my father died — shocked! that I was saying something so personal — so private to someone I had never laid eyes on in my life . . . and shocked too that I was saying something so far from what I was really interested in discussing which was his fingers — where they came from — how they came to look like that — what their ancestry was — whose hands in the family did they resemble — what comments did they arouse — did people always notice them and stare — women especially etc. etc. *but I didn't dare! — god forbid!* as I began instead . . . falteringly . . . hesitantly . . . telling him about my father . . . appreciative that the old fart had just died because now at least I had something to talk about and for this I felt a ray of real gratitude — finally he gave me something I could use . . . finally . . . as I self-consciously . . . falteringly . . . was saying that his death had been completely unexpected . . . it had been so hot I said, with no rain, not a cloud, just day after day of unremitting cloudless heat circling the event like a wall and it hasn't let up I said as I took another one of his cigarettes . . . (so much did I need the comfort of this slim white tube that gave off the kind of solace that could get me through as I flicked it around in my fingers, dashing off the ashes and taking puffs) as I was trying to explain . . . tentatively . . . haltingly . . . that no sympathy was necessary because I didn't like my father any more than he liked me, and anyhow I said, he was still around me all the time because the dead don't die . . . it isn't that easy I told the fellow as I kept staring at his fingers, my eyes glued to them as I told him that since I wasn't really in mourning, he therefore needn't feel sorry . . . here we were I said, two strangers — my father and me, stuck with each other with nothing in common I said, except a few high hopes that it would all work out . . . that something might make it all work out like a little goodwill and maybe some tenderness I said — which is probably the best there is . . . a little tenderness and a bit of genuine goodwill, but that was never in the cards for us — we never had much kindness for each other I said as I glanced at the fellow's somber face . . . as a wild desire suddenly soared up in me . . . a madness you could say . . . to make this fellow smile . . . maybe even laugh . . . some unexpected sudden urge to make the gloomy sad-sack sitting next to me in the neat yellow shirt with the dark horn-rimmed glasses who seemed so serious, so solemn . . . *happy* . . . Suddenly I wanted this fellow's heart to fly — No more gloom! No more sorrow — No more painful heavy-heartedness that was weighing him down so bitterly . . . I wanted to take it all away — *yes!* — as I slid over a little closer and smiled as I inched my hand a tiny bit nearer to his . . .

. . . *as all of a sudden . . . the ghost of Nathan Smollens rose silently up out of the blazing concrete in front of us . . . then sat down on the bench between us . . . and began staring at the fellow with the steady unabashed glare of the dead looking back into life and still hating it . . .* His name was Nathan Smollens I said — a dentist I told the fellow, who worked on small things in wet little spaces with thick heavy hands and a dark-tempered edgy impatience until last Saturday morning, which seemed like years I said, instead of only a week ago.

And since the gloomy fellow with the sad eyes and the astonishing penis fingers seemed to be hanging on every word, I told him how the heart in Nathan Smollens's massive body suddenly gave out as he was running for the bus. Then I told him that his death was so sudden that I hadn't gotten used to even the possibility that this dark mountain, this fierce tank of a man could ever be vulnerable to anything even remotely human, no less to something that would silently tear him to the ground like one of those old trees you see in the forest lying on its side . . .

And since the fellow was still listening like every word I had to say mattered — like I mattered and what I was saying was important . . . suddenly all the hidden inequities and angers . . . all the lurking shadowy discontents . . . all the nimble rage that had been hovering just on the edge . . . like a spigot that hadn't been used for years — a spigot that halts and sputters and then suddenly blasts out its foul orange slime — it all came flying out . . . everything . . . as I began describing the hospital's crowded emergency room last Saturday morning with my father lying on a gurney out in the hall, not even a cubicle for him to die in properly — the almost kindly way he looked at me that day, how he almost smiled as he put up his hand, either to beckon me over or to wave good-bye — I didn't know, I couldn't tell . . . but it didn't matter I told the fellow, because by then it was all too late . . . by then I felt nothing, neither sorrow nor pain nor grief nor fear nor even the smallest sense of loss . . . nothing . . . by then I was as numb as a rock as I stood beside him humming . . . as he lay dying on the gurney.

And as I took another one of the fellow's cigarettes I told him that walking home from the hospital after he died, walking through the park that afternoon past the very spot where we were sitting now, all I could do was beg God not to bring him back — *please!* I kept whispering — *keep him!* I kept praying as the air around me was beginning to lighten with each step I took, and with each step I took the sun was beginning to shine more and more brightly through all the trees — so brightly in fact that I almost couldn't see the gift at the center of all that bright white glaring sunlight — *my freedom!* I told the fellow as I tried to explain, my words suddenly coming fast and easily in that first great flush of telling . . . spilling . . . confiding — that first great voluminous outpouring that binds two souls . . .

. . . my father's stamp on my whole being I said, was a dense thick blackness that was always about to explode, an encroaching darkness I told him, that was always sneaking up behind me — his hand always raised to me like I was a kind of filthy cur . . . this man, I said, who made the earth shake every time he walked in the house mopping the sweat from his forehead with his big white handkerchief and then blowing his nose into it which made the same terse sound as one of those little New Year's Eve tin horns, his only greeting to me a grunt as he'd stare blankly off into space — no words — no smiles, nothing but dirty looks and fierce contempt . . . and if he dared look directly at me — if he dared glance at me for even an instant he'd go wild . . . because it was me I said — just the sight of me — just the sound of me . . . everything I said — everything I did . . . whatever I was wearing — however I was sitting — however my legs were crossed, however my hair was fixed, everything — anything — caused thundering rages every day at breakfast, every night at dinner — my shoes — my shirt, my socks . . . but why the fellow asked — what had I done (as though I had to do something) . . . what could have been the reason (as though there had to be a reason) . . . I never had a clue I told him, except maybe he wanted a son . . . maybe he hated women . . . maybe he suspected I wasn't his child even though I looked exactly like him — had the same nose and hands — had been born into the same house with him where I lived beside him for the past seventeen years, but those were only guesses I told the fellow — all I could be absolutely certain about I said, was that he hated me . . . I infuriated him . . . I enraged him . . . *me* — I was what drove him almost mad . . .

And then one week ago today . . . without a whisper — without a hint . . . without a moment's notice he was gone . . . he died I said, and so did everything around him . . . all his fountain pens lined up neatly in his desk . . . all his pencils next to his little thing of rubber bands — all his suits, all his overcoats, all his socks — all his wide-brimmed Borsalino hats — all his brown wingtip shoes, each pair exactly the same as the next in a straight long line in his closet — everything exactly as it was . . . except the life had gone out of all of them —

they had all become flat lifeless objects . . . except for me . . . I had gotten my soul back from the dead I said as I looked at the fellow sorry — I would have liked a better story I told him as I took another one of his cigarettes . . . as I noticed his sad patient eyes watching every word I uttered with something calm . . . something unhurried — something slow and not excitable like he had all day . . . and this fascinated me because it was so different from Nathan Smollens —

Maybe because my father died only the week before so there was wild new hope in the air . . . maybe because this fellow was quiet and patient and he listened, which was so different from Nathan Smollens — or maybe it was his astonishing fingers that my eyes were glued to the whole time I was talking . . . or maybe because he was dark and swarthy with something sad . . . something cheerless and gloomy about him that made me feel comfortable — even safe . . . I didn't know . . . I could never figure out exactly what it was . . .

three

Then it was his turn — his story as he cleared his throat
. . . His father he said was in his thirties — very hand-
some — the happy-go-lucky type that things always
rolled right off of . . . never a grudge, never a mood,
charming, funny — no ax to grind as he jumped out of
bed on a Saturday morning toward the end of May, the
twenty-first to be exact he said as he kept trying to light
his cigarette against a sharp wind that was suddenly
kicking up . . . fierce gusts suddenly sending the dry
leaves all around us whirling wildly upward, while at
the same time thick black clouds began darkening the
sky as the sad fellow with the astonishing penis fingers
kept striking match after match as the whole city
was suddenly turning an ominously eerie silver like a
strange, unearthly foreboding.

He was twelve at the time — that's how old he was
when he heard the shots blast out — two he said . . .
a terrible sound . . . something you can never begin to
imagine — the second shot seemed like it lasted forever
he said . . . and then a moment later he said he saw his
father stripped naked, facedown in a pool of blood in
the living room next to the piano . . . who shot him
— why . . . why his naked body was facedown on the
floor . . . why his yellow-and-black-striped pajamas were
out in the hall . . . why nothing was stolen — why there
were no fingerprints . . . anywhere . . . ever . . . Oh,

there were theories he said as he finally got his cigarette
lit — all sorts of theories, all sorts of possibilities — was
it a gambling debt . . . was it a case of mistaken identity
— was it a personal vendetta — revenge . . . a botched
burglary . . . To this day nobody knows, which means it
could have been anyone — the FBI, the president of the
United States — you, me, or the guy next door he said
as he shook his head, as a strange half smile curled his
lips . . . such a beautiful smile I remember thinking . . .
making the moment huge — that smile . . . that I stared
at wonderstruck as he was saying something about his
mother taking off — something about being taken to
his grandmother by his father's driver, his smile gone as
he pulled out another cigarette . . . and as he reached for
the matches he added that his grandmother's house, a
tight little run-down dump at the other end of Atlantic
City had that old-lady smell of camphor everywhere,
and since it was nowhere near the ocean, now there
were no more breaking waves he said, which before he
said he could see from every window — hear even in
his sleep . . . no more big front porch he said, where he
used to sit for hours watching the sunlight glittering on
the water . . . no more tasting it on his lips as he'd run
out over the dunes early in the morning to see the sun
come up . . . his own personal ocean that had become
almost a person to him . . . this steady, huge indifferent
mother you could say — gone . . . like his own, whom
he said he still could see in a shimmering gray satin
gown with a diamond barrette shaped like a star in her

long red wavy hair . . . only where was she standing . . . on the stairs . . . in the hall . . . in the dining room . . . it all got blurred in the haze of his father's death . . . everything . . . the sound of gunshots — the diamond star in his mother's long red wavy hair . . . moving in with his grandmother . . . rainstorms — a pool of blood — summer nights, gunshots . . . the diamond star in his mother's hair . . . until finally he couldn't absorb it all — finally he said it all began to seem like some kind of monstrous mistake — all of it some gigantic error

. . . as the pale lady . . . wrapped in a golden shroud . . . loomed up out of the blazing concrete . . . and sat down between us on the bench next to Nathan Smollens . . . the pale lady in the golden shroud that would endure on our bench . . . or on another bench . . . or at the dinner table . . . or at Thanksgiving . . . or at every wedding and every birthday celebration and every New Year's Eve for all the rest of time . . . unvanquished . . .

. . . as he tore out of his grandmother's house day after day, jumped on his bike and went searching for her down every street in Atlantic City all the way from the inlet to the bridge and then back, riding at top speed from one end of the island to the other . . . looking . . . peering . . . going slowly down every alley . . . in and out of every driveway . . . looking . . . looking . . .

The school where he was sent, an all-boys academy run by the nuns of the Precious Heart, had a thick stone wall with a huge iron gate that he said he would hang on every afternoon waiting for her to come — only after his father was shot she never came again — not ever again . . .

For a long time he said he sat in class looking out the window that looked out on the gate watching for her . . . waiting . . . until finally it began to sink in . . . until he finally began to understand that she wasn't coming . . . and when it finally hit he said — when he finally realized that this was the way it was he said he had nowhere to go except to his studies with all the heartache and strength that was in him, and within a year he said he took every prize in the school — math, science, English, history — this little Jew who lived with his grandmother, the only Jew in the entire school, which made the old witch even crack a smile, but he said he hated her so much with her wild mass of thick gray hair and her toothless wild gray eyes whom he planned on killing as soon as he had a minute, strangling her in her sleep or setting her on fire as he turned even more to his studies, and the next year he said he piled on still more prizes, still more honors, and that's how it went he said until he entered the University of Pennsylvania when he was seventeen without too much — a few books, a couple of old photograph albums, and a gold pen that had once belonged to his father . . . The strange part he said as he reached for another cigarette . . . was that after his mother left he said he was always hungry . . . a constant rankling miserable thing that nothing could satisfy he said as he looked at me . . . and I understood . . . this fellow and I were from that whole army of abandoned children . . . we came from the woman in the portrait above the fireplace in the black lace gown whom we could never reach or touch or smell — who was she . . . the woman up there staring down at us in all her pearls and rings and bracelets, her hands folded stiffly in her lap . . . as the sad fellow with the astonishing penis fingers lit both our cigarettes on one match as though there were no fierce wind driving all the leaves whirling frantically upward — no darkening sky glowing in a kind of eerie silver incandescence that kept getting darker and more uncanny, as thunder was beginning to rumble out of the west like the great growling underbelly of the entire universe . . . his dark unshaven face screwing up . . . as great streaks of jagged thick white lightning began flashing across the park as he was telling me that after two years at the University of Pennsylvania, where he was the youngest on an elite team of mathematicians working on that famous monster ENIAC — his whole life changed in an instant he said, because of an aunt and an uncle whom he had never met until the day they offered him a job . . .

Zelda Strong was his father's older sister he said as he finally got his cigarette lit . . . an aging card shark by then he said, with dyed orange hair and a huge diamond ring the size of an ice cube, along with a round gigantic diamond in each ear that she wore all the time, even on the bus . . . And as the heavens suddenly burst open . . . as thick black drops began pelting us like rage coming down in a wild fury — this immensely good omen that something terrible was finally over, and now at last something else — something new and exciting was about to begin as we were sitting there trying to smoke wet cigarettes . . .

Skinny as a rail and hard as nails, he laughed . . . The way she'd spit at policemen who tried to give her traffic tickets he laughed again, as wild torrents were lashing into us like they had teeth . . . curse salesgirls he said, who weren't fast enough wrapping the goods — shriek at waitresses who brought her coffee anything less than scalding, and worst of all he said as he began fishing around in his pocket for his handkerchief . . . the way she shrieked at Uncle Jack, her husband and partner in their chicken-and-egg empire when she was really sore, as Uncle Jack, to whom nothing and no one was sacred, would take the cigar out of his mouth and start whistling while he'd roll his eyes upward toward the ceiling . . .

Aunt Zelda was supposed to have been a chorus girl in the Ziegfeld Follies he said as the rain was beating down on us so hard that the sad fellow with the astonishing penis fingers finally took off his glasses and put them in his pocket, his eyes very different without them — smaller and much more intense as he kept staring at me as he was trying to light a cigarette, those astonishing penis fingers cupped tightly around the cigarette with the lit match deep inside the cup . . . But the fact was, he said as he smiled that swift little glittering smile again as the rain was plastering his shirt to his body so closely that it was impossible not to see the huge amount of hair on his chest (almost grizzly) . . . it was the Jewish follies — not the Ziegfeld Follies he said as the rain was flattening his hair so completely that it looked like he was wearing a thick black bathing cap, but since it was wildly exciting just to be sitting there — something like sitting in the middle of a hurricane because there's something wildly exciting about nature at its worst . . . and since we both were able to see through each other's clothes that by now were glued to each of us like tissue paper, you could say it was a spectacular moment because first of all, there was finally relief from the unbearable heat . . . and second . . . we were able to get a good look at the other as if the other were sitting there completely naked . . .

And she wasn't exactly a chorus girl either he went on as he was wiping his face with his handkerchief as he was staring at my breasts, not blinking . . . she simply swung across the stage in a big pink bell with only her legs showing — legs, he said that were so incredible he laughed as the rain continued beating into us like we were in the middle of a fire hydrant . . . it didn't matter what the rest of her was like . . . not with legs like that he said, as if to say that all you need is one good thing and then everything else is forgiven . . . as if he were really saying, beauty — that certain magnificent gift we're all so hungry for excuses everything . . .

And as for Uncle Jack he said, still staring at my breasts . . . he was a fat jowly man he said, with a big cigar stuck permanently in the left side of his mouth, a rank gambler who spent every waking hour playing the casinos in Atlantic City where the high rollers were treated like royalty he said, as he handed me a lit cigarette . . . especially the Pelican Lounge at the Atlantis he said, where Uncle Jack played the tables every night . . . And then he added that Uncle Jack was orange . . . that his skin was orange because he used a cheap indoor tanning lotion — that his hair was orange because he hennaed it himself which turned it a kind of flaming iridescent, and all his loose-fitting leisure clothes were some shade or other of orange . . . and as the rain continued beating into us — the fierce madness of it lashing into us as if it were made with bits of broken glass . . . nails . . . spikes . . . the fellow with the astonishing penis fingers bent over to bail water out of one of his beat-up old brown loafers as he was saying something about how Uncle Jack started out a concert violinist, while Aunt Zelda, an aspiring opera singer, was making her way in the follies (whichever follies, Jewish or Ziegfeld) to make ends meet — They met, Uncle Jack developed stage fright and Aunt Zelda was tired of swinging in a bell so they got married, retired to a tract of land in northern New Jersey, turned it into a poultry farm, and proceeded to amass a fortune in chickens and eggs — And the reason they wanted to hire this fellow the moment they laid eyes on him he said . . . wasn't because they were a successful, driving, childless couple who wanted an heir . . . or because this fellow was the son of Zelda Strong's only brother, who for reasons having to do with a certain piece of real estate in Atlantic City — a certain *very valuable* piece of prime boardwalk real estate that ultimately became the Majestic Hotel and Casino, which had briefly belonged to Zelda Strong but was mysteriously sold by her brother's wife — this Solomon Columbus's mother, Cissy, without Zelda Strong ever seeing a nickel which immediately snapped relations between Zelda Strong and this fellow's father . . . but, the fellow added . . . this had nothing to do with why they wanted to hire him or not hire him because family ties, an unsolved murder — the disappearance of his mother and all the heartbreak that went with it were all a big yawn to these people — It had no meaning — Nothing did except what could profit them.

To Zelda and Jack Strong, the entire universe and everyone in it didn't so much as exist he said, except for the few random individuals here and there who could serve them, which was the beginning and end of the meaning of other people.

Therefore he said as he bent over to bail water out of his other shoe as the rain kept lashing into us as though it were laced with shards of steel . . . they didn't give a hoot whether he was their orphaned nephew or the man in the moon — they offered him a job the day they met him because he was a crack mathematician he said, who could figure in seconds what most people needed a pencil and a piece of paper for . . . and the Strongs liked that.

It all began during his second year at the University

of Pennsylvania where he invented a game called Poz he said, which he said was a child's dice-and-card game . . . The beauty of it he said as he was rummaging in his pocket for his cigarettes, was that it could be played alone, which made it an instant success, and when he realized this — without wasting a minute he said he sold the game to one of the big game companies, made a bundle, went out the day he sold it, bought a black Cadillac convertible with a bright red leather interior — jumped in, put down the top, and now, with a few bucks in his pocket for the first time in his life, he drove directly to Atlantic City to find the aunt and uncle whom he had heard about but never met he said as the lightning was flashing so close that we could hear it sizzling . . . thunder rumbling immediately on top of us as the wind and rain were making it almost impossible to light a cigarette . . . I ask you, he smiled as he kept pushing his sopping hair back off his face — what made me go out that day and buy a flashy black Cadillac convertible with a bright red leather interior, jump in, and take off in search of these people . . . It wasn't their money he said, or all the diamond dust that goes with it — no he said somberly as I bent over, trying to shield my face from the lashing rain with the bottom of my skirt . . . he was too smart for that he said as he was wiping his chin with his arm — he knew all about that kind of glamour . . . that it was a trap that too easily could eclipse everything, and anyhow he said, money was never the thing that drove him . . . He was a quiet fellow he said, who liked listening to classical music, going for long walks in the woods or going to museums where he could walk for hours gazing quietly at old suits of armor and broken bits of pottery . . . those were the things that drove him he said, and not much else . . . and as he was speaking I realized that it was his calmness . . . that it was a certain peacefulness about him . . . something slow and tranquil as I was beginning to feel him almost as a place where a person could stop for a minute and take a breath, so it wasn't his fingers only, but a certain slowness now — a certain quiet serenity that he was beginning to weave like an iron cocoon all around my jangled spirits, mixed with a feeling that I could trust this fellow — trust even the dazzling little smile he'd brandish for moments that I was beginning to treasure, knowing the whole time that smiles can be tricky — they can be very untrustworthy . . . very duplicitous and conniving . . . but not his . . . his was a quiet smile that I very quickly began to need like it was a prize — almost a gift you might say, that I could earn if I were smart enough . . . funny enough . . . pretty enough — that smile . . . that I was suddenly willing to work my heart out for as I moved a little closer as he was saying how Uncle Jack smacked him on the back that first time they met, and with his big cigar stuck permanently in the left side of his face said, "son, to be a success in life, there's only one thing you need to know, *and that's who to stay away from!*" his uncle laughed uproariously — so uproariously that his uncle started choking the fellow said as he kept pushing his sopping hair off his face as he nodded yes, almost as though he were nodding to himself, as if to say that yes — it was that kind of talk — that kind of organic wisdom that springs directly from the street that was music to him, which he said was why he sat with these people in their cabana on the beach for the next ten days, joined them in their card games every afternoon, went to the Pelican Lounge with them every night where the high rollers, smoke and whiskey altered his thinking so completely that he left the University of Pennsylvania two weeks after he met these people, which meant that he left that elite team of spectacular mathematicians who were working then on ENIAC . . . *the Electronic Numerical Integrator And Computer,* whose initial purpose back when it was first conceived during the Second World War was to compute artillery shells . . . But it turned into something else he said . . . Something unimaginable . . . Something beyond spectacular as it soared out of the Moore School of Engineering at Thirty-third and Walnut Streets — out of the University of Pennsylvania — out of the country and finally out of the world as it roared into history to become what's known today as a *computer* he almost whispered, his sad sorry eyes not blinking as he was looking at me with a look that was almost a confession — That's why I came to Penn, he said — To be part of that team, world-famous by then that was working on that great gray dinosaur — that monster dinosaur he said, that became the miracu-lous little bird that changed the world . . .

So why — tell me! — I asked as I jumped up and stood smack in front of him, barefoot and sopping wet in all that teeming downpour . . . Why, tell me, did you give all that up — Why did you leave the university — How could you! —

I left, he answered, his whole somber face clouding over, leaving only a kind of stony glare as he looked down . . . because I wanted to have a cup of tea and a couple of cookies with people who had known and loved my father — Something that simple he said, as he kept looking down . . .

    . . . *as the pale lady in the golden shroud who had been sitting on the bench between us . . . the pale lady sitting there . . . next to the ghost of Nathan Smollens began to laugh and laugh and laugh and laugh and laugh . . .*

four

As the rain kept pounding us — lashing and beating into us — drenching us to the bone as it kept filling all the gutters along the sidewalks with black little rushing rivers, the sad fellow with the astonishing penis fingers finally stood up . . . his story told, his confessions made — his rage, confusion, and shame now woven solidly into our coming journey across the park . . . westward over Locust Street . . . south down Twenty-first . . . across the street . . . up three marble steps and into my house — an old red-brick Federal with dirty windows, chipping paint on the shutters, and not much furniture. By the time my father died "Trixie" had sold almost everything because she liked having a little extra change jingling in her pockets, and what's more, the house was always cold, even on the hottest days . . . kind of like being deep inside a damp dark cave, or in some old sunless quarter of a dark ancient city where you know no one and never did, where my mother, whom since I was very little I had always called "Trixie," otherwise known as Bea Smollens, would be sitting in her thick red velvet chair beside the window — her tattered old red velvet throne with the big mahogany carved arms like dragon's heads, the only piece of furniture left in the whole upstairs den except for a couple of mirrors . . . By the time my father died she had sold all the sofas and easy chairs upstairs and down — all the little end tables and lamps and chests — even the dining room table was gone by then along with all the chairs and the big mahogany breakfront, which I tried to explain to this fellow — explain the emptiness to him — prepare him for it as the rain began tapering off, most of the fury of it suddenly gone as he took my hand as we began our dash across the park, which meant that finally I was touching those five astonishing fingers as we began running, barefoot, our hair and our clothes smacked flat against us as I was telling him as we were running that it was more a matter of dancing with "Trixie" than talking to her, and even though he'd know how to dance the steps I said, he'd never understand the music they'd be dancing to . . . she wouldn't let him . . . there were too many mysteries he'd never be able to unravel . . . too many secrets . . . too much he could never figure out because she was too unusual — too unpredictable, so he should never argue with her I said — he should just follow her lead — just keep dancing I said, until it all becomes a kind of act which is called survival I told the fellow . . . and then I told him that I had always called her "Trixie" because it seemed to fit . . . and what's more I added . . . she was *spiteful*!

. . . but first a word about his fingers . . . first a word about those ten astonishing things on his hands that I couldn't tear my eyes away from — those wildly flagrant, blatant things that I kept staring at mesmerized . . . those fingers, that seemed so lewd at first — so extreme in what they resembled — so outrageous — almost not even like fingers — almost like this man might have been arrested for some kind of strange exposure . . . and add to this . . . there were ten of them . . . *ten* . . . that he didn't seem even the slightest bit aware of . . . he didn't realize almost, or he didn't seem to realize how outrageous they really were — to him they were probably just his fingers, because who knows if anyone ever dared mention anything to him on this account . . . but (and this is the thing) . . . finally having him take my hand in his as we began our dash across the park . . . finally . . . holding hands with him as we began to run, which meant that I was finally feeling them — touching them — finally having them around my own which I expected to be a monumental moment — a thrillingly exciting start to everything . . . I'm sorry to say was one big zero . . . and this was terrible because I knew the instant I touched them, with that awful knowing — the kind that leaves no room — no hope . . . that some enormous element wasn't there . . . it was missing and this made me sad because I had hoped for magic and there wasn't any . . . I felt nothing . . . no tingling . . . no thrills — no nothing as we went up the three marble steps in front of my house — in the door — through the black-and-white-tile vestibule — through the dark front hall still holding hands, up the stairs and into the den on the second floor where Trixie, who by then was as deaf as a stone, blind in one eye, and had a thin black mustache, was waiting for me with her usual sharp angry look — "High time you showed up Ramona

Smollens!" she snapped from deep inside her tattered dark red velvet throne that was in front of the tightly shuttered windows so that the whole empty room seemed to be sealed in a kind of lightless fog.

"And who may I ask is *that*?" she snapped as she pointed to the dark sad-sack whose disappointing hand I still was holding — odd how you get used to things, how fast they become suddenly no big deal I was thinking as I answered, "Mr. Columbus," not willing to mention his first name because I knew she'd make fun of it.

"Ah ha!" she beamed — "And who are *they*?"

"The Columbuses . . . ?"

"Yes!"

"Chickens and eggs," I answered.

"Ah ha! — Chicken and eggs, I see," she said as she glared at him. "Don't you just love the way those Orientals never flush?" she asked.

"Well, I —" he fumphed.

"Well?" she asked as she turned her glare to me — "As usual your hair's a mess — Long and wet could be very '*oo-la-la*' — But short and wet *is Terrible*! — How many times do I have to tell you to stop dyeing it *Red*! — Just let it grow out in your own dark brown — It's a very good-luck color — Rich — Romantic — Full of mystery — But no! You insist on continuing to *dye it that atrocious Red*! — Why? — That's what I would like to know? Still trying to copy that movie star Rita Hayworth who you love so much — Ha!" she laughed as she continued glaring at me as she blew her nose — "So

Mr. Columbus," she said as she shifted her glare back to the fellow standing next to me — "Did you know that common household dust is composed of *human skin*? — *Well it is*!" she glared at him.

"Realize," she said, "that every time you scratch you pollute the air. I'm not saying never scratch," she said, "I'm simply saying *realize* that when you do you pollute the air we all have to breathe — Now !" she said, "Tell me about yourself," she glared at him, not taking her eyes away from his face for even a second as she continued blowing her nose . . . "I want to marry your daughter," he grinned as he looked at me.

"You want to *What* . . . ?"

"Marry your daughter," he said again as he kept grinning. We were standing in the semi-dark of that cold bleak upstairs den in front of the long French windows, each window with its own double set of white painted shutters, tops and bottoms kept permanently shut and latched as though Trixie was trying to shut out every-thing — the world — light, time, and everyone . . . "My daughter is barely seventeen years old," she snapped — "How long, may I ask, have you known her?"

"Four hours," the gloomy sad-sack with the dark horn-rimmed glasses answered as he looked at his watch to make absolutely sure — "The happiest four hours of my life," he added as he looked at me.

"Very touching," my mother scoffed as she kept blowing her nose into the little rumpled Kleenex — "If you remember, which I sincerely doubt," she scoffed again, "come back and talk to me in ten or fifteen years — Now!" she said as she looked at me — "show this *'Mr. What's-His-Name'* to the door," she ordered with a flick of her hand, as though her hand were a magic wand that could wipe this *Mr. What's-His-Name* and every word he uttered completely off the planet.

. . . but I didn't show this *Mr. What's-His-Name* to the door — why I don't know, and it wasn't that I liked him or didn't like him . . . that was the strange part — In fact it had nothing to do with that — or with his disappointing fingers for that matter either, that had suddenly become like ten dead stones that I wasn't particularly interested in touching anymore . . . The fact is — I didn't know what it had to do with or if it had to do with anything — Maybe it was just because he was sad and I understood this . . . or because he was calm and I found this fascinating . . . or because he smiled every time he looked at me . . . or because of the way he listened to every word I had to say like every word, every syllable was important . . . or maybe it was because he wanted to marry me the minute he laid eyes on me . . . or maybe it was because there was something about him that was needy and in pain that he didn't try to hide and I understood this . . . so instead of showing him to the door, which would have been the end of it, I silently led him on tiptoes down the stairs, through the dining room and kitchen . . . through a little door in the butler's pantry that led up a narrow flight of wooden stairs and into the suffocating attic at the top of the house, where the last shards of gray, rain-lashed light were lying across the dusty floor up there like long gray panes of slanting glass . . . And in that roasting place that was covered in thick heavy dust and cobwebs everywhere, where every discarded object of a lifetime was whispering its sad little muted song . . . my grandmother's chipped china plates and platters . . . her coffee cups with their broken handles . . . my mother's old evening gowns from when she was glorious . . . piles of strange beach towels, a broken bicycle — dolls . . . my old dollhouse . . . broken chairs — a box filled with *National Geographic* magazines from my father's heyday as a dentist . . . my collection of old movie magazines with Rita Hayworth on the covers . . . and under one of the eaves, a tattered old red velvet sofa with thick white stuffing coming out of both the arms . . .

"I've got my period," I whispered . . . "Get a towel," he answered as he began taking off his shirt.

five

Not long before that, a few weeks before my father died . . . maybe three . . . there was another dark-haired boy on another scorching summer afternoon, when the leaves on the sidewalk were beginning to curl from all the heat . . .

His house was near the end of Ringold Place — a narrow block of small orange stucco houses, each with three orange stucco steps in front where he was standing . . . staring at me . . . and I stopped . . . who was he . . . I never knew . . . what was his name . . . I never asked . . . I just went with him — that was all . . . and in the sweltering heat of his messy room at the top of that stifling little house with all his papers and books and dirty socks and underwear strewn everywhere — that room . . . thick with the heavy smell of him . . . that foul sweet thick male smell all over everything — the bed, the pillow . . . and afterward . . . as I was watching him staring at me like he was stunned . . . silent . . . not one word exchanged be-tween us as I was putting back on my clothes . . . I was thinking only that I felt nothing . . . nothing . . . something in me wanted him — that was certain — something in me craved and desired him the same as he desired and wanted me . . . but like a wild beast that was too huge — too overwhelming to be captured, no less ignited . . . the beast remained hidden . . . silent . . . leaving me completely untouched . . . unscathed . . . the only feeling . . . envy . . . for how easily he could have so much pleasure.

six

The rain that hit while we were sitting in the park that day took the end of summer with it — the insufferable heat was over — the long sweltering summer that had taken Nathan Smollens . . . gone, with autumn hanging golden in the wings . . . something crisp and blue all across the sky with a lot of hope.

They say that people marry to right all the errors of their childhoods, therefore they say they marry to make all their dreams come true, and if that's the case, if that premise is correct, they believe that suddenly everything becomes possible . . . like happiness . . . an old-fashioned idea that floats like a big pink cloud, its shadow over everything as the sad fellow and I stayed up in the attic for the next four days and nights; who knows why we stayed up there that long — who knows why this Mr. Columbus kept calling it "making love" — who knows what "love" had to do with anything, or what "love" even was . . . maybe we were just trying to take a little stab at something — *life*! maybe we were ready in spite of the fact that I didn't like him all that much . . . his fingers lost all their charm by then and nor did I especially like the way he looked, something too greasy and dark like he was dipped in oil . . . In fact, I don't know what there was that attracted me or if anything attracted me — or if we just kind of fell into staying up there out of boredom — it's hard to tell what prompted it, this life we began up in the attic, but I'm sure it had nothing to do with "love" because as I've said, I didn't know what "love" even was except for a deeply tender feeling I had every now and then for my mother, anguished and mixed with a terrible kind of sympathy, which made me want to hock everything I owned and give all the money to her but that was the last thing in the world I felt for this fellow — During those four days and nights there were no anguished feelings mixed with any kind of sympathy . . . No sentiments or any kind of tenderness . . . nothing like that was going on up there — nothing at all . . . During those four days and nights it was all about this fellow's excitement, and although he probably thought that I was excited too — I wasn't . . . For me it was about my effect on him — that was all . . . For me it was about discovering an allure I seemed to be developing in all the dust and cobwebs of that hot little stifling attic as he'd leap on top of me . . . and then again . . . and then again . . . like a great mountain cat, his cheeks flaming — his whole body like a furnace . . . and do it . . . and then do it again . . . and then again . . . and even though I felt nothing — not a twinge — not an inkling — not a hint of anything — nothing . . . I was excited by the excitement I was able to arouse in him — the madness I was able to create in this dark gloomy fellow . . . an excitement that came as a bit of a shock because my sense of myself was that I was anything but exciting . . . In my opinion I wasn't clever . . . I could never make decent conversation, I was too shy, which made talking a curse . . . and I wasn't pretty either, but none of that seemed to matter, and because it didn't matter I never let on about not feeling anything down there because in the first place I expected better days . . . sooner or later I expected I'd feel what I was supposed to feel, what was natural and normal to feel, like I expected sooner or later that I would somehow be like all those fabulous women in all those movies I grew up on — swept away, responsive and remarkable — I was sure of it, and for that reason I was able to stay hopeful and expectant, like a child at Christmas who knows with certainty that there's a Santa Claus . . .

. . . and yet . . . on the other hand . . . what if — god forbid . . . it didn't happen . . . what if — god forbid it never happened! . . . what if — god forbid better days didn't come . . . never came . . . what if I never felt anything — because maybe — what if god forbid — I was . . . "frigid" . . . which would mean that there was something wrong with me — that I was damaged . . . and if I was damaged . . . down there — if that was the case, god forbid . . . it was the last thing I'd ever want this fellow . . . or any fellow . . . or anyone . . . to ever know about — the disgrace that I couldn't measure up — that I was a dud — the shame — the humiliation as Rita Hayworth, the pinnacle of every magnificent quality — of everything exquisite in a woman flashed by in a striking red flamenco dress, tight across the hips, low-cut with thick heavy ruffles — *Rita Hayworth!* who stood for something so deeply irrefutable within life itself — so utterly indestructible within the whole big scheme that she was on all those bombers during the Second World War because to men — all men *she was life Itself! because Sex is life Itself . . . Rita Hayworth . . .* as she was bang bang banging banging banging her heels as she was clap clap clapping clapping clapping her hands above her head as she was laughing . . . *at me* . . . mocking . . . jeering . . . taunting because she knew . . . and I knew she knew . . . that I was a failure, as the sad fellow and I sat wrapped in beach towels talking casually as though no catastrophe was brewing just beneath the surface of this new little life we were living up in the attic . . . no secret tragedy I was trying to hide . . . no heartbreak that was beginning to emerge as I was smoking his cigarettes, one after another . . . taking deep puffs and fanning myself with an old movie magazine with Rita Hayworth on the cover as I was telling him that lately a worrisome thing had come over Trixie . . . Lately I said, as I took another cigarette, she had begun talking to herself in mirrors I said, and whatever she said made her laugh so wildly that now whenever she'd see a mirror, after a moment of saying something into it, some secret thing she'd whisper behind her hand she'd begin laughing uproariously I told him . . . and this went on I said, until finally she'd start laughing without having to say anything into it . . . just the sight of a mirror — any mirror, but especially the big one in the downstairs hall brought on something so wildly hilarious that she'd double over in gales of laughing so hard that sometimes she'd have to dab her eyes, and since there were still plenty of mirrors all over the house because she hadn't sold those yet, she was very busy, so either she didn't notice I was missing I told the fellow . . . or else she pretended she didn't notice — either way, every day for those four days I'd drop in on her for a few minutes while the gloomy fellow ran out for cigarettes and this was enough to assuage whatever feelings of responsibility she might have had toward me, feelings that were minimal anyhow . . . because the truth was, she was too busy with the mirrors and didn't want to be disturbed.

. . . and as I was reporting this whole little saga of loneliness and insanity . . . I noticed that this Mr. Columbus was wiping his eyes on the back of his hand . . . weeping maybe . . . tears . . . for me . . . I couldn't be sure . . . because it easily could have been the dust up there or an allergy to spiderwebs . . . or that yes . . . he was truly moved by the madhouse I was describing that was my home . . . and although he didn't say so as he stopped wiping his eyes, wiped his nose on the back of his hand and cleared his throat, I concluded that it wasn't an allergy — I concluded that his heart went out to me and even though he didn't say so, I truly believed he understood, and I concluded as we were sitting there that being understood was more important than even being loved . . . as he switched the kaleidoscope to a whole other configuration as he began telling me about enormous gambling debts his father had, a woman his father was connected to who was connected to the mob — the property in Atlantic City again, which became the spectacular Majestic Hotel and Casino, followed by his suspicion that his grandmother was a numbers writer, and I countered by telling him that Rita Hayworth had had electrolysis to move her entire hairline back an inch . . . that she yawned all the time and when she wasn't yawning she was half asleep but it was her hands I told him — in the end most of all it was those remarkable hands and the way she did the flamenco . . . and then I told him how I'd gazed at her spellbound as I'd sit in the back of the Egyptian Movie Theater . . . wonderstruck . . . *Rita Hayworth!* . . . all a man had to do was breathe on her and she'd instantly become a sex-crazed powerhouse with a wild frenzied passion that led to immediate ecstasy . . . as a whole new wave of desire suddenly seized this fellow as though even just the subject of Rita Hayworth — even just the mention of her name made him leap on top of me . . . and do it . . . and then do it again . . . and then again . . . so how could I tell him . . . how was it possible to tell him that I felt nothing . . . nothing . . . that I was dead down there . . . completely dead, which was beginning to make me think that maybe yes . . . I was "frigid" — although "frigid" is far from what it was — frozen maybe . . . or damaged, or tied in knots . . . something tragic that I didn't know how to even understand as he began talking about the murder again as he lit two cigarettes — then something about his father's girlfriend . . . her name was Minnie Slater, whom a detective by the name of Maurice Sunshine suspected right from the start, like the detective suspected everyone including, or maybe most especially, this fellow's father's driver . . . as the fellow looked at me with a strange, faraway look . . . and as he was taking a deep drag on his cigarette he said, almost as though he was talking to himself . . . that there are certain things a person can never accept because the event is too huge — too devastating so the tragedy remains forever outside the senses in the form of information — a fact . . . knowledge, that's never really taken in — never really absorbed — it just floats he said, on the terrible question — *"why?"* . . . as he described again the sound of the gunshots as he lit another cigarette . . . again — his father facedown in a pool of blood . . . again, the police flooding the house "like a pack of swarming crows" . . . the rabbi running in, whom he said had never ridden on the Sabbath before in his life . . . what the weather was like that day — the new yellow leaves outside on all the trees . . . His mother standing beside the front door in a blue robe with sunlight flooding the whole downstairs . . . her disheveled wild red hair with that look on her face that he said he'd never forget — *"that look!"* he said, that was all that was left . . . *"that look"* and as he lit another cigarette he said that the deepest search in a person's life, the one thing central to every human being . . . is to find one's mother — not just the mother of your flesh and soul he said . . . or even the lost mother, but the image of a strength and of a wisdom that's greater even than the hunger . . . as he quickly, almost seamlessly moved the kaleidoscope again as he started making wisecracks as he told me how Uncle Jack worshipped, not God — but every poultry buyer from every grocery chain who ever came to a food convention in Atlantic City . . . how Uncle Jack would wine and dine them, *"with nothing but the best,"* he said, which had a secret meaning, *"with nothing but the best"* meant that Uncle Jack would slide the poultry buyer's room key across the table at the end of a lavish feast at some swanky restaurant . . . the key to a suite that came complete with the best call girl in Atlantic City . . . for the chicken-and-egg buyer from the Great Food Company in Tulsa, a black hooker with her hair slicked back and her black satin skin so oiled up that she was as sleek and as shiny as a gorgeous piece of ebony . . . for the poultry buyer from the Amadeao chain in Seattle, a Japanese knockout in high black boots with whips . . . for the poultry buyer from the Orlando Market Company, a black six-foot beauty in white vinyl shorts and big white vinyl boots . . . and two little Chinese twins dressed up as boys for the poultry buyer for the Lewiston Chicken Soup Company in Lewiston, Illinois, with never a word exchanged — no discussion, all of it tacitly understood that it was all being taken care of by Uncle Jack — *everything!* . . .

And as Mr. Columbus described more seamy details of his company's sordid operation without the slightest change of expression . . . or blame . . . or judgment . . . as though this was just a little courtesy — some little

favor to encourage business . . . I stared at him in disbelief . . . aghast . . . appalled — *horrified*!

. . . but why he asked with an expression of blank bewil-
derment on his dark melancholy face — this is the way it
is — this is the way things are — this is *life*! he laughed,
oblivious to the fact that I was completely horror-stricken
as he began describing one particular "black goddess" in
a red satin kimono as he lit a cigarette . . . her hair slicked
back he said, with her sculptured nails just so . . . so much
chutzpah — so regal — so haughty — with the kind
of confidence that could drive a man completely wild
— turn him into a sobbing beast howling on all fours
because it's all about confidence — Confidence! he said
almost as though he were talking to himself . . . And as I
listened . . . horrified — appalled . . . who is this man —
this awful creature I picked up on a bench in Rittenhouse
Square I was thinking as he kept rambling on and on
about a certain kind of commanding performance . . .
these great fakes he said — the way they'd strut like a
bunch of female impersonators . . . like a bunch of men
in drag putting on a terrific show — such good theater, he
said . . . like an opera without any music, he was laughing almost like I wasn't there . . . again almost as though
he were talking to himself . . . as I listened . . . stunned
— horrified . . . my mind going blank in disbelief . . .

    and yet . . . in another way . . . as I listened . . . I was
becoming excited too . . . thrilled . . . by his compassion
for these women . . . thrilled . . . by his compassion for the

poultry buyers . . . thrilled . . . by the way he understood without any condemnation — there was no censure . . . no criticism . . . as I kept listening . . . just human needs . . . and the acceptance of these needs and this excited me because it was so different from Nathan Smollens — so different from my father's raging tirades with his furious admonitions of right and wrong looming over the dinner table every night in his buttoned-up nine-piece suit even in the dead of summer, shrieking red-faced about "a certain cousin" who once "fornicated" with someone in an alley . . . as I looked at this dark melancholy fellow . . . this naked hairy man sitting next to me with his glasses off — this Solomon Columbus . . . thrilled . . . by the hint of liberation he was offering . . . thrilled . . . by the hand he was extending in the dark by his sorry acceptance of the human beast — this Solomon Columbus — who could pay a "black goddess" in a red satin kimono to give him all the pleasure he could have so easily . . . then stick it back in his pants and leave . . . and this excited me because it was humanity speaking . . . Not rules — Not the rantings of a rigid fanatic who had wrapped himself in a shroud of hollow morality that would take everybody down with him . . . all of us . . .

. . . as I kept listening . . . and as I kept listening the more I heard . . . and the more I heard the more I wanted to hear . . . and the more I heard . . . the more wildly . . . almost irresistibly drawn to this fellow I found myself becoming.

seven

We were married in a stifling little room at the top of City Hall four weeks to the day after my father died.

I wore a gray straw hat that day that had a little gray straw flower, a gray cotton dress, and black stiletto heels, and for the occasion, Mr. Columbus wore a new black double-breasted suit with black silk lapels, almost a tuxedo — a black silk bow tie, black patent-leather loafers, and a white shirt that had tucks all the way down the front, making him look more like a headwaiter than a groom . . .

I had never seen him with his hair slicked all the way back like that . . . slicked back so far and so flattened down that it looked like it was painted on . . . or with a shave so close that his cheeks had a kind of pink incandescent radiance, as if something way down deep underneath the skin, some essence of his soul, had suddenly sprung outward and was shining through . . .

He was happy . . . I had never seen him happy . . . I had never seen him so full that he looked like he was about to burst . . . this sad melancholy fellow with the dark horn-rimmed glasses, swarthy and oily with his thick fat penis fingers laced in mine . . . formerly the most morose downcast individual I had ever laid eyes on in my life . . . Formerly he walked around like he was carrying something dead, something he was taking to its grave and that's what I was used to — to that distant, disconnected look, with something distracted about him, like a veil was over his whole soul — a veil that separated him from all the rest of life, cut him off from everything except the people rattling around inside . . . his demons — all of them all scratching around in there trying to get out — the murdered father — the father's driver, the grandmother . . . the mother who ran off . . . so whenever I'd see it — that look, as soon as I'd see it slant across his eyes I'd sit down beside him and pull my sweater off, as new wild heady power feelings would sweep over me because I knew my body excited him and this excited me as my breasts suddenly felt like they were growing . . . as though they were suddenly becoming big wild things — huge and powerful as he was staring at them — so powerful in fact that they could do almost anything that arms could do . . . even hold him — even rock him . . .

And as he was watching me giving him this gift — my nakedness . . . complete and absolute . . . he'd charge out of his miasma, jump on top of me with renewed gleaming life — miraculous life . . . all of life miraculous again . . . because this gift — my nakedness would change the immense unhappiness he carried — this gift, my nakedness, would touch the terrible weight that was always pulling him under as he'd be lying on his stomach on the floor with his head in his arms in that universal posture of sorrow . . . and as soon as I'd see it — the moment I'd see him like that I'd sit down on the floor beside him and pull my sweater off because I wanted to make him happy . . . I wanted to give him all the pleasure that I could . . . that's all I wanted . . . that was all I ever wanted . . . as he'd roll over, at first still in the depths of something huge and terrible, but if I just kept sitting there . . . quietly . . . steadfastly . . . slowly his spirits would begin to lift and then that awful weight he carried, that terrible price he was always paying and paying until his whole life began to seem like one huge unknowable, un-understandable debt . . . some mysterious debt that felt like it would never end no matter how much he paid and paid and kept on paying and paying but if I sat down beside him on the floor and pulled my sweater off . . . slowly . . . it would begin to ease . . . I could see it easing as he'd pull me over . . . and that would make me happy because it meant that I had won another round against *her* . . .

. . . *the pale lady in the golden shroud . . . the pale lady that was always sitting next to him . . . the pale lady that was always breathing on him . . . always reaching out to grab hold* as he'd roll on top of me, press me into him so close that I could barely breathe as he'd start up like a great chugging huffing locomotive . . . huffing and chugging and puffing and huffing . . . and then suddenly he'd come tearing down the tracks and then . . . it was all over — done! while I was lying there . . . still feeling nothing . . . not a twinge — not a whisper . . . as he'd fall asleep behind me . . . his soft sleeping business curled up against me like a warm pink baby.

eight

Our honeymoon in Atlantic City as I floated between two lives, childhood on the one side in my mother's house . . . and on the other — womanhood, and the rugged discovery, little by little of what that meant . . . as I sat beside him on the beach watching the ocean loll forward softly, break into little waves, and then back off . . . walking with him on the boardwalk in the blazing afternoon, his fat penis fingers wrapped solidly around my own, only now they were only fingers, nothing more . . . finally I had become so used to them that now they were nothing more than things that held a knife and a fork, wrote with a pen, buttoned and unbuttoned a shirt or held my hand so tightly that it was almost as though he was trying to squeeze me into him as we walked along the beach at night, almost happy in the comfort of each other's presence . . . noticing how the moon looked so much like my mother . . . almost as though she were talking to me — whispering to me about my hair . . . her crooked finger pointing to it in a long white stream across the water under all those billion blazing stars . . .

. . . thinking about her waiting for me in that empty upstairs den . . .

. . . thinking about her sitting in her tattered old red velvet throne in front of the windows with the white shutters that were always closed and latched . . .

. . . thinking about her one blind eye that looked like

a gray marble with deep pink circles like thumbprints around them both . . . thinking about her thin black mustache . . .

. . . thinking about my old bed at the far end of the second-floor hall, the dingy organdy curtains in there, gray and stiff and dirty . . . thinking about my gloomy little bathroom — almost too gloomy, almost too heart-breaking to take a bath in there but I was longing for it, my heart breaking for how sad and dim and sweet it was as I sat with him — this Mr. Columbus on the veranda of the Hadden Hall Hotel, sipping long pink drinks from long thin frosted glasses . . . as I looked at this man — my husband wondering what I was doing there, in that strange place, Atlantic City instead of my old living room on Twenty-first Street — longing for that bright glare of white blinding sunlight that flooded the entire room — longing for those ugly purple ottomans, the two big tattered old yellow chairs . . . the lamps that all had scorched white shades . . . the crooked tables with books under some of the legs . . . and under the two long living room windows that looked out on the street before she sold it, an old green sofa where I used to love to just sit and look around . . . all of it over now . . . gone . . . The time had come for me to move on as though I had been pushed by some great invisible hand because of that musty dark front hall that stank of Nathan Smollens's stale tobacco mixed with her perfume, that sickeningly heavy blood-and-flowers smell she seemed to emit from every opening — even her mouth, even her nose . . . all of it collecting in the stairwell behind the steps that finally became too much . . . finally the whole house . . . finally even the street and all the houses on it . . . finally even the sycamore trees that lined the sidewalk with their odd tan-and-green-mottled skin like staunch guardians of some half-remembered dream . . . the drugstore where Dr. Bruno kept peering around corners to see if someone was nipping suppositories out of the jars; the hunchback who polished the brass knockers up and down the block with his bag of rags sitting on his hump while he was polishing . . . the dry cleaner, the grocery store, the flower shop — all of it that was always my terrain — my place where I used to tear around on skates, throw rocks on a chalk frame on the sidewalk — jump rope, ride my bike, gallop on my invisible horse . . . and sat one day on the curb mourning my dolls that I didn't play with anymore . . . they were over . . . done . . . and wondering as I was sitting there . . . what there would ever be that could ever possibly take their place.

Rittenhouse Square, the park where Mr. Columbus sat down on the bench beside me, was more like the private garden of some immense and marvelous home. The fountains and sculpture and sprawling grassy lawns surrounded on all sides by all the great old city mansions was the pinnacle, the golden belly button from which everything in the city radiated in bright shimmering banners of green waving trees, gleaming red polished doors, cobblestone streets, and red-brick sidewalks, with our house two blocks over, which brought it down two rungs to a more modest, simpler, gentler, more smiling neighborhood . . . Maybe the whole world is full of such places. Street after street of small narrow houses with the first-floor windows the largest, their curtains peeping out like white lace underwear . . . the second-floor windows smaller — the third-floor windows even smaller still . . . and finally the little fourth-floor attic windows, too small to let in enough light even at twelve in the afternoon — that progression of window sizes that gives a sense of grace to all those little city houses that finally get to smell of too much living — too much going on, like the narrow red-brick Federal on Twenty-first Street that had finally come to an end for me, and although I would never look back on those years with ease . . . I longed for my mother with a crushing kind of terrible sorrow . . . longed to see her laughing in all the mirrors . . . longed to climb into bed with her, head-to-toe . . . hug her legs . . . kiss her bony knees while she rambled with her eyes half closed about voodoo dolls and magic portents — about casting spells and spirit life actively going on inside of closets while I rubbed her feet . . . back when I was happy, really happy, when I was close to her in that miraculous time of youth . . . the promise then that was everywhere . . . on everything . . . all of life miraculous then — all of it . . .

Tell me, Mr. Columbus whispered as he'd throw back the covers and grab my leg . . . do women lust? — I mean, does it pound in them — you know, the way it does in a man — a man'll stick his thing in anything, mammals are mammals, he said wistfully, but are women like that? — I have to know, like I have to know exactly what it feels like for a woman while she's doing it he whispered as he began pulling up my nightgown, his business as hard as a junior kosher salami as his thick penis fingers were curled so tightly around my breasts it hurt . . . tell me he whispered — why do women like to dance? he asked as he rolled on top of me — men like to dance because it's the first step to getting in, but why do women like to dance he whispered, his business like a fat snake thumping up against my thigh — tell me why women like to dance — I have to know like I have to know exactly what it feels like when I put my thing in you — does it feel like you putting your finger in my mouth — is that what it feels like? . . . take your time he whispered — then, very slowly — very carefully, explain exactly what's it like as your ecstasy begins he said as he pushed his insistent business into me like you'd manage your hand into a too-tight pocket trying to get at some change . . .

Remember that big black hooker I once showed you a picture of he said as he closed his eyes and began smiling softly as though he were in a completely other world — a world I couldn't begin to even imagine — a world I had no knowledge of . . . the one in the red kimono, he said as he started his climb . . . the one with the skin so oiled and gleaming that she was like a piece of magnificent shining ebony . . . when I asked her these questions she told me that she used to hate the way that people had to "pull themselves all around — this way and that," how clumsy and messy with all that "scrambling and jamming" she said . . . but then she said, once that feeling begins it just keeps building and building till bang — *you come to a head . . . you burst as waves of ecstasy keep rolling over and over you and then you kind of black out* . . . tell me, he whispered, does that sound familiar — is that what it's like, I have to know, he whispered as he pressed me so close that I could barely breathe as suddenly he came flying down the tracks — made that little sound like he was being stabbed and then sank down on top of me as I was thinking as I was lying there that even though the red-brick Federal on Twenty-first Street was only a couple of blocks away, somehow it seemed the distance was enormous, so enormous that I was finally safe . . . finally . . . safe . . . from Nathan Smollens . . . dead or alive . . . who was still pounding around in there somewhere in his yellow satin bathrobe like a zombie whose legs don't bend as he just kept coming . . . coming . . . fearless and malevolently silent . . . in a kind of trance that you couldn't rouse him from . . . not even if you screamed — not even if you threw something at him and ran . . . I wanted tell my husband this as he was climbing on top of me again . . . I wanted to say that from the moment Nathan Smollens walked in the door he started yelling . . . at her . . . at me . . . even before he took off his hat — even before he hung up his coat . . . his rage sucking up all the air — taking up all the space and I wanted to say that I never knew why . . . maybe he didn't either . . . bad luck maybe . . . maybe he was crazy — maybe something chemical in the blood I wanted to tell this man who was chugging on top of me again . . . huffing like a giant locomotive like I wanted to tell him about the sense of worthlessness I was drowning in . . . I wanted to say that thanks to Nathan Smollens I always felt shabby in a shabby dress with shabby hair and shabby shoes . . . everything shabby . . . a shabbiness I could never shed I wanted to say, so desperate was I to be rid of these feelings that hung like dirty gauze all over everything because the dead don't die . . . it isn't that easy I wanted to say — we're not empirical creatures . . . we fly with our past on our wings I wanted to tell this person — my husband, this man — this stranger pounding on top of me . . . chugging and huffing . . . as he suddenly let out that little scream . . . and then collapsed . . . folding on top of me like a big crumpled balloon . . .

So tell me, he asked — how was it for you he smiled as he rolled over . . .

. . . but instead of whispering any of this — instead of uttering a single word . . . instead of breathing even the smallest hint including the fact that I felt nothing . . . not a twinge — not a whisper . . . instead of daring to break the shell that all of this was smoldering in I smiled as I whispered *great!* . . . because I was afraid of losing him.

part two

now

one

Marriage for Mr. Columbus was like a window shade that suddenly shot up . . . His dingy apartment in the old Belgravia Hotel got a new white coat of paint, new lamps — new green silk drapes that looked like shimmering long green evening gowns . . . a big new Persian rug for the long front hall, plus a new little wife who would fix a button, administer his vitamins, make him interesting things for breakfast, like Canadian bacon on a Kaiser roll — make sure his shirts were pressed exactly the way he liked, and wake up beside him every morning, rain or shine, with a loving smile . . . A new little wife who came complete with thick lips, dark eyes, dyed red hair the same color as an Irish setter — big power breasts — various smells, arms to hold him, and a body he could jump anytime he wanted, and this great change of events created a constant Cheshire-cat grin on Mr. Columbus's formerly gloomy face, a huge semi-permanent grin that took hold like a tree that drops its great taproot then and there, and suddenly begins to flourish . . . For Solomon Columbus marriage was the end of aloneness, the end of sorrow — the end of his long and terrible winter as he stepped into the light.

From the beginning, all our pots and forks and dishes became things of the utmost interest to him . . . As soon as we were married he began buying all my clothes, his thick fat penis fingers picking carefully each woolen skirt, each pair of slacks — each sweater . . . his thick fat penis fingers carefully pulling a black silk suit from the rack — each pocketbook, each belt — nothing was too trivial . . . nothing too small or inconsequential as he burrowed himself more and more deeply into all the details of our life, finally even selecting my bras and panties, even my slips and spikes . . . everything receiving his complete and absolute attention; it was as though he dived headfirst into the deepest inner workings of some exquisitely detailed tapestry, and was making his way.

Dinners on the weekend with friends . . . the power of routine . . . the sweetness of comfort, and even if he didn't like the people we were having dinner with — dates made months in advance, it made him happy to just be part of something, to finally be on the inside — to belong to a pleasingly ordered life that began to march like a little soldier, correctly and in tune as he quickly became attached to even the dullest, most unimaginative, most boring people we were moving with . . . it almost didn't matter who they were, he began to crave their companionship as the circle of genial everyday life continued to expand — the gratitude of being peacefully entrenched in an easy chair . . . the power of fresh-squeezed orange juice — the majesty of big bowls of flowers everywhere . . . the joy of having someone nearby to look after him, tell the silent woman in the starched white dress, a woman so light and shadowy that her footstep was never heard, exactly how much starch to use — what to prepare for dinner, how to turn back the bed as we went out . . . to parties . . . to the movies . . . theater . . . then home again to do it as many times as he wanted with everything gleaming silently in the hovering darkness . . . everything humming with erotic promise, so that for him there was no adjustment to married life, but rather a wondrous leap into paradise, as a whole new confident quality crept into this formerly gloomy person . . . Mr. Columbus was happy because he had exactly what he wanted . . . It was that simple because he was that simple because men are that simple . . . but not me . . .

For me nothing was humming with erotic promise — no wondrous leap . . . no paradise . . . as my secret tragedy, my heartbreaking inability — my humiliating failure between the sheets showed no signs of change . . . And as I'd look across the table at him every night at dinner, incomprehensible feelings of desolation would sweep over me . . . everything had become so slow . . . so strung out . . . so tedious . . . as though life had somehow slipped into another gear — grinding and pulling like baseball on TV where they keep repeating the same play over and over and over . . . each time slower . . . and slower . . . and slower . . . and slower . . . I wanted to go home . . . I wanted my old bed . . . my old pajamas . . . I wanted to get under my old covers in my old room and just stretch out . . . I wanted my mother . . . I wanted her to scratch my back while she told me about charmed hat pins and the healing powers of urine as I watched his thick penis fingers reaching for the little silver bread-and-butter knife to butter his roll as he grinned his toothy Cheshire-grin again as he began to cut his meat . . . watching him slowly taking a bite . . . watching him slowly chewing . . . watching him slowly swallowing . . . slow . . . so slow . . . everything . . . going so slowly . . . then grinning his toothy Cheshire-grin again as he was slowly taking a long drawn-out sip of wine . . . what happened to all the gravity — the pull . . . why had the gathering momentum of life — the speed — the excitement come to a screeching halt the minute I married him as he'd sit in the sofa after dinner not saying much because there wasn't much to say . . . not anymore — the stories had all been told as he'd nod off into his regular little after-dinner doze, his head dropped forward, the evening paper fallen from his hand, too tired to do much more than wake up half an hour later, get into his blue cotton Brooks Brothers nightshirt and his blue leather Brooks Brothers bedroom slippers, go into the bathroom to brush his teeth, take off his bedroom slippers, get into bed, leap on top of me like a wild animal — make that noise like he was being stabbed . . . and then roll over almost asleep before his head had hit the pillow as I'd stare into the darkness all around me . . . wondering if this was it — if this was all there was . . . as I'd lay there watching the thin white curtains moving softly in the breeze . . . like ghosts from happier times.

two

Okay then I vowed to tell him everything — I vowed that
I'd come clean starting with the heartbreaking fact that in
bed I never felt a thing . . . not a whisper . . . not a twinge . . .
nothing . . . ever . . . which I should have told him from
the very start like I should have told him then that I never
understood why he kept calling it "making love" because
I never understood what "love" had to do with anything
or for that matter what "love" even was . . . I should have
told him then that in my opinion "love" was just a word,
nothing more, just one of those vulgar things that people
say in order to say something instead of having the courage to just shut up because even if there is such a thing,
it doesn't come from the heart but from the head . . . in
acts of concern for the other person — in acts of genuine
kindness toward that person . . . in acts of sacrifice because
love means sacrifice, which in my own way I was trying
to do by faking my heart out in bed, because aside from
wanting to give him as much pleasure as I could . . . I also
wanted to appear fantastic . . . I wanted to seem like one
of those fabulous creatures right out of all those movies
I grew up on — all those epic romantic myths, luxuri-
ous and sweeping . . . with Ava Gardner . . . or Elizabeth
Taylor . . . or my own beloved Rita Hayworth who could
all be swept away just by being kissed so tenderly that
a hungry passion immediately began to flare up — but
more than that . . . much more — I wanted to build up
his ego, I didn't want to hurt his masculine pride because

if I told him the truth — that I felt nothing and never did, he would automatically assume that it was because of him and this would leave him wide open to every woman under the sun because he would develop low self-esteem and low self-esteem is an open invitation to any predator with even one ounce of the hunt so, needless to say, I had to make him think his business was so big and so powerful that it could not only satisfy every woman who ever lived and breathed but like Plastic Man who could stretch himself around corners . . . slide through keyholes — stretch all the way up the side of a building up to the twenty-seventh floor and even stretch across the street and into a restaurant to open a can of beer for a handicapped person . . . I wanted him to think his business could do as much and even more . . . stretch around corners too . . . slide through keyholes — stretch up the side of buildings and even stretch across the street and into a restaurant to open a can of beer for a handicapped person . . . instead of the awful truth that he was a speeding locomotive with a formidable power that nothing could stop as he'd leap on top of me like a wild beast . . . and then . . . like a train that comes shrieking around the bend so fast I was never able to even catch the smoke . . . he'd crush and flatten me . . . make that little noise like he was being stabbed . . . and then roll over dead.

. . . but I never told him any of this . . . of course I didn't . . . because in the first place I didn't know how — not anymore . . . because in the first place telling the truth ended for me when I was twelve years old and discovered that by lying to Nathan Smollens . . . my soul . . . my whole life force . . . my spirit — even my will to go on stood a fighting chance.

. . . twelve years old, when I discovered that by saying anything I wanted . . . making up anything — *Anything!* like telling him I was at the library after school studying instead of the truth, which was that I was sitting in the park with a friend making the person sitting across from us yawn . . . or that I was talking on the phone at night about my homework, instead of the truth which was that I was talking to a boy . . . or that my teachers praised me all the time or that I made the hockey team or that I was captain of the glee club when in fact I was with a bunch of friends at the diner across from school smoking cigarettes and laughing . . . so if I could muster the courage to just keep telling them . . . lies — all lies! with a dead blank face, my eyes staring straight at him without blinking, and even though it made me sick at first — even though at first it made me wretch with fear, almost throw up . . . if I wanted my spirit to survive that house where there were so many hardships and humiliations — if I wanted my life force to endure . . . my soul — even you could say my will to go on I had no choice — It was the only way I had to fight the rages that would come flying out of him at the drop of a hat . . . over nothing . . . all the time . . . and not just at me but at her too if she said something he didn't like and sometimes even at my grandmother

when she was over for dinner so in the beginning I'd
take a deep breath in — hold it . . . and because I'd be
shaking like a leaf from the sheer terror of not only
lying — but lying to my father . . . I'd have to swallow
all my feelings, keep gulping them down like they were
handfuls of twisted nails, until I was nothing more than
a piece of slick bright shiny machinery that could say
anything — spiel off anything . . . *anything!* except what
was true which I had to hide at any cost — protect with
everything I had . . . and if I could — if I was able — if I
had the moxie I'd own the world and I knew it! and that
was thrilling . . . So thrilling that very quickly I was able
to manage my fears enough to stare smack at him . . .
twelve years old as I'd look him dead in the eye as I'd start
reeling off giant whoppers from the moment he walked
in the door and the more I did it the easier it became
until finally I could spew out anything that came into my
head — fast — cold-bloodedly, and finally without even
a trace of remorse — Finally I could do it with not even
the slightest pang because it was a matter of survival . . .
the survival of my whole life force — my spirit — my
soul and survival came first, "principles" in those days
were a luxury I couldn't afford as I kept advancing inch
by inch up the ladder of duplicity — swiftly — easily . . .
until finally without so much as a hint of conscience,
because conscience is love and since a child can forgive a
father anything except not loving her . . . my conscience
was clear as I began moving into a whole new realm of
so much wild lying — so much blatant dishonesty that

my lies were becoming something else . . . something more . . . almost like a wild new art form — something like a whole new kind of soaring creativity — my own form of raucous self-expression . . . imaginative! — limitless wild and *free* . . . as a great new elation began to take over — an enormous heady thrill like a painter must get when he's creating his masterpiece as I'd look straight at him night after night as I began weaving great tapestries of pure deceit — curtains and bedspreads and slipcovers of lies . . . all lies now without blinking an eye . . . Finally, without giving it a second thought whole flagrant madnesses would come flying out of me at the drop of a hat . . . *because now the truth belonged to me AND ONLY ME . . . Mine! Nathan Smollens . . . MINE . . . So Ha! Ha! Ha! on you because now my soul — my spirit — my very will to go on living — what I felt — what I cared about and what I thought were all safely hidden now inside a great protective shell of lies! . . . all lies . . . get it! Nathan Smollens . . . So Ha! Ha! Ha! on you . . . Ha! Ha! Ha! Ha! Ha!*

And just to be doubly safe . . . Just to tighten the screws a little more — Just to perfect this new excitement of lying my head off anytime I pleased I began branching out . . . Next I began lying to Trixie who, as much as I loved her I held some grudges against her too . . . Then to our maid Mae whom I secretly despised because she was always asking questions, always poking — snooping . . . Then to a few people in my class at school whom I had always secretly detested because that's how I began to show my rage — by lying like a snake to whoever enraged me — to anyone who enraged me . . . until finally, I could lie even to people I didn't hate . . . even to people I liked . . . until it didn't matter finally who I lied to as I crossed over into that last most treacherous stage . . . which was when I started lying to anyone who would listen — cabdrivers, people next to me on the bus, waitresses — salesgirls, friends at school — anyone . . . because finally it had become easier and much more fun to lie than to tell the truth.

. . . but there was a danger . . . and I knew it . . . I knew I could forget where I put what I was hiding . . . it could get lost . . . as though I had slipped my foot into an all-encompassing boot that was so infinitely protective and so comfortable that finally only the boot existed — my foot had gotten lost in there somewhere . . . like the truth . . . which became a fading little flicker way out on the horizon . . . some distant little glimmer somewhere far far away . . . almost like a dream I couldn't quite remember . . . and in losing it I lost myself in a vast glass forest that had no markers — not a road sign — nothing to guide me . . . not anymore . . . and so in bed with Mr. Columbus . . . when my secret tragedy began to unfold . . . when my heartbreaking failure between the sheets was becoming unbearably clear . . . when I was finally forced into accepting that I was a block of wood down there — a switch that didn't switch on — that I had a terrible disability, it was a logical leap — almost you might say a natural one for me with my history —

with my familiarity with lying, the ease with which I could pull it off — the enthusiasm — the grace . . . to become a complete sex phony — a total lying sex fraud in bed, which is what pornography is . . . lies . . . all lies and since that's what I understood that's what I became and I became a good one too — so good in fact . . . that I was beginning to feel like I was someone else stuck in someone else's life — not mine . . . which was fast becoming a life that was worse than meaningless.

three

Every evening, while Mr. Columbus was taking his little after-dinner doze — his head dropped forward, the evening paper fallen from his hand, I'd walk out on our terrace — light a cigarette, take a deep drag and then lean up against the red-brick wall staring at the smoke as it was curling slowly upward . . . and noticing . . . as it was curling . . . how sometimes it looked exactly like Nathan Smollens . . . like his thick bulldog face with that strange blank stare . . . his eyes all glassed over with not seeing as he kept coming toward me with that stiff-legged rigid walk like a zombie whose knees don't bend as it keeps coming . . . coming . . . as I'd scream for her . . . every night . . . screaming for Trixie as I'd run into my bedroom, slam the door and lock it with him on the other side pounding to get in I'd like to tell my husband . . . this man — this Solomon Columbus sleeping on the sofa in the living room because the dead don't die I'd like to tell him . . . it isn't that easy I'd like to say as I'm looking down into the street that seems a million light-years below . . . and wondering as I was looking . . . if I jumped . . . maybe I would fly.

part three

her

one

The first time I caught her was out on the terrace while Mr. Columbus was taking his usual little after-dinner doze, and although I couldn't see all of her . . . that is, I saw only the tips of her white satin shoes in the shadows over near the living room door, my first suspicion that something was going on was the smell of perfume that was everywhere that night . . . as though our whole apartment had been fogged in sex.

How she got in — who let her in or if she had a key I can't say, but that she was in my apartment looking for my husband was very clear because as I've said, I smelled her perfume everywhere that night — in every room — in every corner . . . heavy, powerful, and so thick you could almost see it — almost touch it . . . It hung in the air like clouds as the realization . . . very quietly . . . was beginning to dawn on me . . . *that yes . . . my husband had someone* . . . and as I gazed in at him sleeping on the sofa . . . all the recent — odd events . . . all the strange new goings-on . . . like the phone ringing late at night — every night . . . and when I picked the receiver up, the person on the other end clicked off and not just once or twice . . . but countless times . . . night after night . . . accompanied by a strange new look on his face when I'd ask him about it along with a new reluctance to talk — an unwillingness to come clean about anything — even where he went for lunch . . . which was all beginning to add up . . . two and two were beginning suddenly to make four . . . *that yes . . . he had someone all right* as I stumbled backward, fell against the terrace wall, and gasped . . . as though my heart were suddenly blowing up inside of me . . . reeling . . . as though I had just been punched by some great invisible fist that had suddenly sprung out of nowhere.

. . . and then she was gone . . . as I looked back into the shadows where only a moment before I had seen the tips of her white satin shoes . . . now I saw nothing — smelled nothing . . . that heavy gardenia perfume — gone . . . everything — vanished . . . leaving only tormented feelings I didn't know how to begin to even grapple with, except to understand that only a moment before there had been a woman on our terrace in white satin evening shoes — an audacious cold-blooded calculating *slut!* who would dare . . . *dare!* — sneak into *my home* wearing so much heavy gardenia perfume that there could be no mistaking the fact that she was there *to fornicate with my husband* . . . with bare shoulders too I suspect — and no underwear . . . in some slithery slinky sequin gown . . . her hair just so, with long red-painted fingernails . . . looking for Solomon Columbus . . .

And why not! — Why wouldn't every woman on earth be looking for Solomon Columbus! — Why wouldn't every woman who ever lived and breathed be looking for Solomon Columbus as I glanced back into the living room to see him still sleeping on the sofa . . . his mouth dropped open . . . the evening paper fallen from his hand as the devastating realization, swift and terrible as I was standing there was that yes . . . whatever love was . . . whatever weird and terrible thing . . . I loved this man with his dark swarthy face and his ten fat penis fingers that were once so magnetic, so exciting back before my secret tragedy began to unfold . . . back when all I wanted then was to hold them . . . feel them — put them against my cheek and in my mouth — Back when a line between what he wanted and what I wanted didn't exist, like it doesn't exist now between him and this new black cloud that's hovering over everything — This force — This woman who must be so wild and so exquisite — so free and so passionately in love with him that she'd risk everything . . . *everything . . . of course! . . . and why not! . . .* because even though he's swarthy, dark, and skinny he's not bad looking — No! Not at all — This noble savage with something classy — Something decent, something clear of prejudice and he's not impressed — rich or poor, high or low it's all the same . . . and nor does he need much . . . or ask for much — or want much . . . All he wants is what he's entitled to — *His Life! — Flying Around Him All In Color! . . .* and what's more . . . He's rich . . . *Money! — The Great Aphrodisiac!* which all by itself turns them all inside out . . . makes them do anything . . . *Anything! . . .* become audacious little scheming whores — all of them . . . hungry . . . reckless . . . even going so far as to slip into another woman's home in the middle of the night reeking of so much heavy gardenia perfume that I had to cough — *Money!* . . . which makes them all come crawling out of the woodwork sniffing the scent of every dollar bill like he's sniffing the scent of what's up their skirts . . . And what's more, although he has a brain when it comes to mathematics, chickens and eggs, when it comes to women he'd slurp after anything that would even *look* at him — *Anything!* because he can't resist even the sleaziest come-on from even the sleasiest little *slut* . . . and nor does it pay to confront him about it either because even if he were caught with his pants down he would admit *nothing!* — *ever!* — *to anyone!* — "I know how to keep my mouth shut," he'd say as he'd smile . . . or ever blame himself for anything — "Blame being the lowest form of thinking," as he'd put it and then he'd throw in Uncle Jack's philosophy — *"that the most important thing in life is to know who to stay away from,"* almost as though he were warning himself . . . except he's the one who's gotten himself all tangled up with the worst kind of vile vermin — the worst most despicable kind of predator that lives and breathes, which is the kind of slime that goes after another woman's husband, which to my mind is a special kind of loathsome . . . a special kind of despicable . . . but then . . . in all honesty . . . who can blame him . . . with a faulty piece of merchandise like me.

In bed, where the body tells the truth and it tells it ruthlessly . . . his business is always a gloriously blazing part of him — a magnificent flaming source of so much pleasure all the time while I fake everything . . . every time . . . all that moaning — all that thrashing — all that throwing my head this way and that as though I'm adhering automatically . . . almost instinctively you could say, to some ancient unwritten law that says that pleasing a man in bed is the first rule . . . the beginning place . . . without which there is nothing.

two

The second time I caught her was on one of those nights when he'd roll over, ask me "how was it for you?" and then be snoring before I had a chance to begin the whole litany about his flaming kisses, etc. etc. — his magic touch, etc. etc. — what an incredible lover, etc. etc. — the lights going off and on in my head, etc. etc. — his unbelievable "business," etc. etc. etc. . . . except on this particular night, which as I've said was the night I caught her for the second time . . . just as I was about to begin my usual spiel — my usual long-winded slew of lies . . . all lies . . . a rage, that took the shape of terror because it was too afraid to be a rage suddenly came flying out of me like a murder of screaming crows as I bolted out of bed — rushed to the window, threw it open wide — stuck out my head . . . and as I looked up at all those billion blazing stars — all those blazing lights up there, terrifying and terrible, flung from that same gigantic hand that flung them on our honeymoon except back then there still was a glimmer of hope . . . there still was a glimmer of a prayer that I wasn't defective . . . *except I was* . . . *nothing changed* . . . *not a thing* . . . as I began shouting out the window that I still felt *nothing! — Nothing! — I was still as numb down there as a stone* . . . *Numb!* . . . What a hideous joke I began laughing uproariously — almost screaming with laughter until I didn't know whether I was laughing or crying . . . and nor did I know who I was laughing at either, or who I was screaming at or who I was shaking my fist at as tears were streaming down my face . . . was it at my beloved Rita Hayworth . . . or at Ava Gardner . . . or at Ingrid Bergman — Ginger Rogers — Marilyn Monroe . . . or maybe it was at all of them, all my Saturday-afternoon goddesses who all were swirling on mirrored stages in white chiffon telling lies . . . all lies . . .

And what about all those cowboys too — What about all of them sitting around the campfire smiling while they strum their guitars, happy because they know that on Saturday afternoon there's always a happy ending . . . They know the good guy always wins . . . always gets the pretty girl, their passions exploding immediately into rapturous ecstasy every time with never the need for any foreplay . . . or any struggle . . . ever . . . or ever a quirk . . . or any kind of hang-ups . . . or anything weird . . . nothing! — the cowboy never wears high heels and ladies' underwear . . . Frontier women never scream at cowboys . . . throw things — chop off all their hair in a frenzy or slam the kids with frying pans . . . only endless smiles of never-ending happy endings as they flash their big white perfect Chiclet teeth as they gallop off into the sunset because everything always works out for them *but not for me* — *No!* — For me things haven't worked out at all . . . Not even the most ordinary normal things that are supposed to work out I'm shouting out the window — Not even the most common simple everyday things that every human being is entitled to expect, which is to feel a simple desire that automatically turns into a hungry passion that can be satisfied one-two-three so that afterward I can laugh and sleep and dream *except I can't . . . because I don't work down there — I'm stuck!* so why break my heart by letting me believe that marriage makes a person happy . . . that being in love is wonderful . . . that the good guys always win or that living "happily ever after" really happens because it doesn't which is why people cry at weddings because they know deepdown that weddings are a kind of funeral because that's when it all comes to a screeching halt . . . everything . . . the story's over . . . the end of dreams . . . the end of hope . . . happiness, a fading memory as you cross the "shadow line" and step out of the enchanted garden as the prison gates clang you in once and for all so why not tell us this all you lying Saturday-afternoon goddesses in all your white chiffon — Why not tell us that life breaks your heart and there are no happy endings . . . Why not tell us that in order not to be fainthearted cowards — in order not to be spineless jellyfish, why not tell us that what we need is a little *Courage! — Strength!* . . . Why not tell us that what we need is to be *Brave!* — Not the bravest person in the world but brave enough to bear the unbearable . . . like watching Trixie secretly hiding the few little dollars she could pinch from Nathan Smollens, stashing them in her blue satin stocking box in the top drawer of her bureau . . . *brave!* . . . as I watched him find them as he pushed her aside as he started rifling through all her drawers . . . as he kept coming . . . coming . . . every night . . . night after night . . . with that blank stare in his glassy eyes . . . his legs not bending as he kept coming . . . coming . . . as I slammed my door and screamed for her and kept screaming for her and screaming because the dead don't die I wanted to shout over to my husband — it isn't that easy I wanted to yell to him . . . we fly with our past on our wings I wanted to holler to him sleeping there so soundly — so all tucked into all the covers only now I wouldn't dare, *god forbid!* because now he has someone — a perfect dazzling famous creature who unlike me needs no help with *anything* — none whatsoever I'm sobbing as I tear out of there . . . running through the hall . . . running . . . running . . . through the living room — out onto the terrace and over to the little wall — naked, no slippers . . . my dyed red hair all wild and disheveled as I look down into the street below . . . suddenly terrified by the urge to jump . . . a wild terrible urge . . . an urge that felt like it had a mind all its own as the street began rising slowly like a strange freight elevator that only moments before seemed a million light-years below as it began whispering come on Ramona — do it — jump — come on — jump Ramona it was whispering — jump — come on as I got down on my hands and knees and started crawling as fast as I could go away from the terrace wall . . . away from that urge . . . tearing across the cold stone terrace floor into the warmth of the living room — stark naked and on all fours crawling across the living room rug, through the hall . . . past the kitchen . . . tearing along on my hands and knees heading back to our bedroom as fast as I could go to wake Mr. Columbus so he would pull me up from the floor, hold me for a couple of moments, throw on some clothes, and then go down into the street with me to walk it off . . .

. . . and that's when I caught her . . . over in the shadows . . . again . . . just past the kitchen door — in those same white satin shoes, all right . . . in a long white strapless gown all right, with one thick rhinestone strap going over the other shoulder . . . her hands on her hips — sneering . . . with her head thrown back . . . reeking of so much gardenia perfume that I had to cough which made her look straight at me for a moment . . . as she began tapping the heel of one of her white satin shoes very fast like all the great flamenco dancers tap their heel when they want someone to come running — I knew because I had seen them do it a million times as I sat in the back of the Egyptian Movie Theater watching . . . spellbound . . . mesmerized . . . only who was she . . . she looked familiar — that much was certain . . . maybe it was that tall black whore whose picture he once showed me back when we first began — maybe she was back . . . or maybe it was another one of the ones he mentioned . . . I wouldn't be surprised . . . addiction is addiction . . . as I inched up closer . . . squinting . . . to get a better look because the light wasn't good in that tiny hall . . . it was neither night or day — that odd time right the before dawn when according to Trixie "spirit life abounds with its fine magic mist over everything" . . . as I kept looking . . . squinting . . . maybe it was one of our friends — I hear friends (or so they're called) are treacherous when it comes to husbands . . . or maybe it was someone at the club — a waitress or the coat-check girl because I've heard that coat-check girls are usually sluts . . . or maybe she was one of his secretaries . . . it was definitely someone I had seen before — of that I was absolutely certain . . . as I crept up closer still . . . so close now, that if I put my hand out I could touch the tip of one of her white satin shoes as I kept squinting . . . because as I've said . . . the light was bad in there, the hall was small, and it was still dark outside so that the kitchen window didn't give much light . . .

. . . as I suddenly heard myself gasp as though my gasp were coming from the other end of the world . . . echoing . . . echoing . . . the agony of all the ages as I recognized *of course! . . . the form! . . . the hair! — those hands and nails . . . and then . . . the face! — my god! . . .*

. . . as I sank back into the shadows, crouching naked and terrified . . . as I let out a yelp like a wounded animal . . . *Rita Hayworth!*

part four

war

or

"arm to arm on the rim of the well"

(Federico García Lorca)

one

Rita Hayworth or no Rita Hayworth! I hissed from the shadows where I was crouching naked on my hands and knees — How dare she barge in here like this with that big, wide, flat-lipped smile . . . Sneering — Well, we'll see who has the last sneer I hissed as I began to tremble, either because I was so furious . . . so intimidated . . . or else because I was so excited to see something that astonishingly beautiful — that gorgeous in front of my kitchen door even though she was there in bold defiance of every law of decency — *of course!* because she was there to fornicate with my husband *of course ! — why else?* — but fornicate with my husband . . . laugh at me — sneer . . . still . . . she was so beautiful . . . so magnificent . . . and no one's immune to that including even me as I kept gazing . . . stunned . . . by that head of thick red wavy hair cocked back and over to one side . . . by those big exquisite hands like the flippers of some fabulous sea creature . . . a seal or a penguin or a lobster maybe . . . with long tapered perfect fingers . . . and exquisitely manicured long red fingernails placed flamboyantly on her hips . . . I understood as I kept staring at her why my husband was so madly . . . so insanely in love . . . never mind that she was maybe the most famous pinup girl in history . . . never mind that there was a stencil of her on all those bombers during World War II . . . never mind that a photograph of her went up with the first atomic bomb they exploded over Bikini Atoll, making her, you might say, the poster girl of World War II — never mind all that . . . It was because she was schooled in all the "womanly arts," which you could tell in a glance was the thing that made her so fantastic . . . so mysterious — so dark and treacherous even though there was something dead about her, like there's something dead about any woman who goes after another woman's husband . . . something not quite there — not quite alive about them when you look them in the eye, and even though they know all the tricks, like how to be the perfect hostess who speaks perfect English, perfect Spanish, perfect French, and perfect Hebrew . . . of course! . . . like she also knows how to dress . . . and how to dance . . . and how to shimmy and how to cook and serve and pour, and above all . . . how to drive a man insane . . . it was obvious . . . by just one look — that she's the kind who turns instantly into a lascivious sex maniac without a need or a wish or a desire of her own except the desire to please . . . the desire to accommodate . . . because most of all . . . in one glance . . . you could tell that she was pure passion that could instantly explode into wild fulfillment every time which is the ultimate weapon of course that she uses to snare them — chew them up and then spit them out . . . oh boy! I was up against some formidable opponent . . . because one glance and you could see that in bed she was abandoned, always hungry and passionately satisfied with nothing cheap, nothing tawdry . . . nothing vulgar . . . quite the contrary . . . She was regal, elegant, and classy to the point of even being haughty with that certain aloofness you could say, which is the hallmark of real sex appeal — right, Rita? I whispered . . . that certain haughty coolness that says she doesn't care even if she does as she stood there gloating because she knew, and I knew she knew . . . that I could never measure up . . . In every way she was utterly superior down to even her teeth, which now I could see since she had begun to laugh out loud . . . at me . . . her head thrown back with her mouth wide open which gave me a chance from my position on the floor to see them all . . . every one . . . which fascinated me because there were so many . . . with not one capped or broken — or any missing . . . not even a wisdom tooth . . . and not one filling either — nothing! . . . so ha! ha! ha! Nathan Smollens — Oh! how you would love to get a look in there wouldn't you . . . but too bad I chuckled — mole on you old boy . . . My father, the mad oral surgeon of Rittenhouse Square — the great pull-out artist of Philadelphia — They came from all over didn't they? — No distance was too great to have the one and only "Cave-Man Smollens" yank . . . the little grip he'd get on the tooth with those pliers, a fast little sip of orange juice, and then he'd zero in like an old bald eagle swooping down for the kill — No mercy in his profession, no mercy in anything that came across his path — oh no! he didn't know what the word even meant . . . Crimes in the family, those secret atrocities that nobody on the outside ever finds out about are crimes of vanity I whisper . . . Those grotesque family sins that no one on the outside hears one word about are sins of arrogance and unspeakable conceit I whisper up to her as I gazed at her pencil-thin eyebrows and her thickly curled mascaraed lashes . . . so thickly mascaraed that each little lash stood out like a thorn as she stood there waving like a gigantic banner all in pink and gold and peachy white, her long red wavy hair tumbling past her creamy shoulders that were the purest . . . the whitest, the most glowing shoulders . . . something like the shoulders of an angel or a god . . . and yet . . . as white and as gleaming and as golden as she was . . . as luminous and radiant . . . there was something equally as dark and foreboding about her too which made her even more exciting . . . even more mysterious and dangerous like a dark mysterious dangerous city like say Paris maybe or maybe Madrid . . . with dark brown vapors swirling all around her that smelled like the inside of an enormous shell that echoed the whole wide wild sea . . . the whole wide wild enormous sea . . . the sea . . . yes, I whisper . . . but never wash I was instructing her from where I was crouching naked in the shadows . . . oh no, and never apologize either Rita I was whispering, because you're what everything in the entire universe hungers for I whisper — *everything!* I whisper again . . . so awed was I by this vision of abject exquisiteness waving in front of me — this being of such raving magnificence that I too was caught in her magic net . . . I too was snared . . . I too couldn't take my eyes away . . . they were glued to her . . . all of me was glued to her . . . so dazzled and so overwhelmed was I that all I could do was stare . . . dumbfounded . . . like a bug caught on flypaper as it looks, not blinking . . . at its doom.

two

*. . . but I can't love Rita Hayworth . . . I can't let myself . . .
I mean I mustn't . . . not even a little . . . not even for one
second . . . not even secretly . . . which is my struggle . . . to
automatically love my adversary . . . instead of automatically hating her . . . wonder why*

three

But he's Mine! — Dark angel of destruction or poster girl for World War II! — This dark swarthy grease-ball belongs to Me! — His slicked black oily hair belongs to *Me!* — That purple birthmark on the inside of his foot is **mine!** — *Mine!* . . . Like those ears are **mine!** and that mouth is **mine!** and all those teeth belong to *Me!* — Everything about him — Every hair — Every mole, every toe including of course those ten fat penis fingers even though they've begun to get on my nerves — even just the sight of them has begun to disturb me but never mind all that. They still belong to *me* — *Me!* because I'm his **Wife!** — Did you hear what I just said — *Wife!* I shout up at her . . . So Rita Hayworth! I seethe in bold defiance — Now it's *"Arm to arm on the rim of the well!"* . . . Because no one — and I mean NO ONE! can invade another woman's life and get away with it because to invade another woman's life is to declare *War!* . . . and everybody knows that the first rule of war is to know exactly — precisely — who the enemy is . . . So Watch Out! Rita Hayworth — You've shown yourself you lying, conniving low-life bitch and make no mistake, I may be down but I'm not Out! — Far from it I glared up at her . . . as I'm remembering a summer afternoon and a bench in Rittenhouse Square where a man named Solomon Columbus sat down beside me, offered me a cigarette, smiled and then whirled me — not her — on a magic carpet up to the attic of my mother's house . . .

Me! — *Not Her!* where we spent the next four days and nights and even if she'd be better for him . . . because of course she'd be better for him because who am I — nothing but a dead block of wood — a clock down there that doesn't tick . . . a bag of lead that can't get off the ground it doesn't matter because he still belongs to *ME!* . . . *ME!* So I'm warning you Rita Hayworth, I whisper . . . *Rita Hayworth or no Rita Hayworth! — Dark angel of destruction or poster girl for World War II . . . this is the last time you pop in here — get it?* . . . because if you ever dare pop in here again like this . . . I'm warning you . . . I'll kill you I whisper in hot muffled tones so as not to wake Mr. Columbus who was only in the next room sound asleep.

four

... sometimes I think Nathan Smollens might have even liked me — who knows ... I say this because he used to take me to the movies with him every time he went even if it was only for half a movie ... or even if he had already seen the movie twice ... it didn't matter ... nothing mattered except our going ... and always without exchanging a single word for the whole ride over and the whole ride back ... but for that little bit of time while we were in the theater watching his surly grinding rage was distracted ... for that little bit of time as we sat in the dark together eating caramels, I got two while he had three — there was a pause in all the misery ... then the movie was over and that's when the whole thing started up again as he'd glare at me, his eyes bulging like two black bullets ready to fire like he wished me dead so he would never have to look at me again ... only why — what did I do ... or don't you have to do anything — as we rode home in stony silence ... not one word spoken ... not one look exchanged ... nothing

five

Before I caught her the second time, that is, before that fateful night in front of my kitchen door when I was forced to warn her about the repercussions that would follow should she ever *dare* — *Dare!* turn up again, before that night . . . from time to time very joyful feelings would come over me as though from time to time I were madly in love with my husband, and that's when I would be back in touch with only what was good in him. What was calm and sane. I would think how brilliant he was . . . how well informed — how steady, with a real genius for simplification and a complete lack of pretensions, or any kind of snobbishness. Here was a straight-shooting fellow, or so I thought (ha!), with nothing fake — nothing devious, nothing sneaky or conniving, and at times like that there was nothing annoying about him either, nothing boring . . . I saw no trickery lurking in those dark shifty eyes — no hint of treachery, no greedy aggressiveness as he'd grab the last piece of chicken off the platter, utterly indifferent to anyone else . . . At those times even his snoring which could be tumultuous, the fact that he never told me what he was thinking . . . never let on . . . never gave a clue — just a flat dead smile that covered everything as he'd begin to whistle . . . or his love of money — *"Ramona! It's God in circulation!"* he'd whisper with a wild glint in his eye — or his endless morbid obsession with his father's murder . . . or his fascination with the chief detective Maurice Sunshine, whom he still had lunch with regularly — Suddenly none of that bothered me — In fact, when I thought I was in love with him nothing did . . . For those fleetingly precious moments when the best in both of us came soaring out of all the boredom and suspicion like some exquisite bird in flight . . . a hawk or an eagle, it was like walking out into the sunshine again after a hospital stay and becoming part once more of that one big beating heart of all creation . . . that one big soul of the whole entire universe that hovers just above the sidewalk as I gazed in infinite gratitude at the whole big autumn afternoon — the trees — the sky — the clouds . . . happy as I'd walk through Rittenhouse Square filled with a wild sense of joyful freedom because love is freedom . . . Maybe the only freedom there really is . . . *(or is it the need to love . . . some extreme wild card in the whole big deck of human cravings that's greater even than the need to know who you're loving or even why)* . . . but when it would come over me like that . . . that feeling of falling madly in love with him — my husband, Mr. Solomon Columbus . . . suddenly I'd start dwindling . . . shrinking — almost disappearing . . . while he'd start puffing up . . . bigger . . . and bigger and bigger . . . until he'd become almost saintlike to me . . . almost a majestic queen who ruled the entire universe with his eyes half closed — almost a mammoth Egyptian god bigger even than the giant floats in the Thanksgiving Day Parade — some kind of great "almighty" whom I couldn't do without for even five minutes . . .

And that's when it would happen — That's when troubling thoughts would begin assailing me . . . because who was I . . . nobody . . . nothing . . . just some little undeserving ant clawing its way up to the foot of this giant monster-king . . . a little nothing bug who wasn't pretty enough . . . who wasn't thin enough or flamboyant enough . . . or exciting enough or smart enough or charming enough or funny enough to deserve to even be in the same room with this looming husband-god . . . And even worse . . . terrible feelings of jealousy would begin to overtake me and even though this was nothing new, even though this torture started long before I caught *her* — long before I had any evidence — long before our first encounter that night out on the terrace there was a strange uneasy feeling almost from the first moment we moved into his apartment in the old Belgravia Hotel across the park . . . nothing concrete . . . nothing I could put my finger on . . . just an uneasy worrisome feeling . . . a suspicious feeling . . . like something was up . . . like something was going on . . . like something was different like his way of not being completely there anymore . . . hiding . . . or something like that — something different in his whole demeanor . . . like not jumping me every five minutes anymore . . . or asking me all those dirty questions anymore about what it's like to be a woman like he used to ask me all the time . . . or not coming clean about where he had lunch that day . . . with an evasive look in his eye . . . which fed directly into my gathering suspicion about those women who were like fever blisters that never completely go away . . . that are somehow always there . . . lurking . . . whether you see them or not . . . like that "ebony goddess" in the red satin kimono whose naked picture he once showed me proudly . . . or those little Chinese twins he used to tell me about dressed up like boys . . . or that Japanese "knockout" in big white high-heeled hooker boots and tight white vinyl hooker pants with her perfect yellow backside sticking out — who where still always lurking — still always hovering as they'd stroll that slow sexy amble like the queen of England trying to lure him back into their web of secret tricks . . . their web of *"knowing"* . . . that promised an ecstasy I could never even remotely begin to imagine . . .

six

You're crazy! — Completely out of your mind! — How long have we been married? — Eleven Years! . . . In Eleven Years I haven't so much as even *looked at Anyone!* . . . *No one!* — *Not from the moment I laid eyes on You!* . . . *Don't you know* — *Don't you understand that You're the love of my whole Life* — *You! Don't you know that* . . . *Those women are all Ancient History!* . . . *Women from another time who meant nothing Then!* — who *mean Nothing Now!* . . . And anyhow . . . with them it was *strictly a mechanical act that had nothing to do with Love!* — *Nothing to do with feelings!* — Nothing to do with who you get up with the next day and can even still stand *to look at!* — It was like squirting shaving cream on a dog's *Nose* . . . *Carcasses!* he said . . . from Another Time . . . Another Life . . .

. . . but I didn't believe him . . . not one word did I believe . . .

Back in the early days when Mr. Columbus used to tell me everything . . . all his secrets . . . how terrified he'd get at the idea of going to bed with a woman — and why? — because of his birthmark — that huge wine-stain blotch that covered his whole right foot and half of his right leg almost like a scarlet sock that went almost up to his knee that he was sure would revolt anyone who saw it — afraid he'd be reviled for it — detested and then abandoned the way he imagined his mother and his grandmother reviled, detested, and then abandoned him because of it . . . It takes a lot to put yourself out there he'd say — It's about as hard as it gets! but since you can't strip yourself of yourself no matter how humiliating or loathsome — on his first trip to Paris, in one of those sleazy Left Bank cheap hotels that cost thirty cents a night, he put himself "out there" with a young black prostitute — his first "ebony goddess" as he put it, and in that first wild explosion filled with all the terror and ecstasy of so much desire, Mr. Columbus's soul was forged.

When things were going along, for the most part all of this . . . Mr. Columbus's past — that first "ebony goddess" and all the ones that followed whose skin he said, was like "black burnished pearl," it didn't bother me. For the most part I was able to put all of them into some kind of reasonable place, which is its own kind of sanity — reasonableness . . . and for the most part I possessed that kind of reasonableness — that kind of sanity . . . But from time to time things sprang up that created suspicions . . . hints . . . clues . . . then terrible doubts would begin to assail me and that's when I'd become confused . . . On the one hand I sensed that something was going on with him . . . and on the other I thought that maybe he was right, maybe nothing was going on . . . maybe I was crazy — mad — out of my mind like he said . . . but no matter what he told me, when those doubts would begin to assail me, that's when a distrust of every woman he looked at coupled with an insanely jealous hatred of every one of them flared up to consume every minute of my waking life . . . as things kept happening that he wouldn't explain . . . like the smell of perfume around the collar of his shirt . . . like the phone ringing at all hours of the night that he made me answer . . . and when I did — every time . . . the caller clicked off . . . and then it would ring again . . . and then again . . . and every time I answered the caller clicked off . . . again . . . and then again, which made me suspect those women were back full-force because that's who Mr. Columbus was — a man who never got over anything . . . Not his father's murder — not his mother taking off . . . and not his passion for prostitutes — Creatures he said he could never figure . . . never know who they really were — what made them tick . . . or what they thought of men like him . . . adding that they were women he could study his whole life and still never understand and what Mr. Columbus couldn't understand he couldn't shed . . . Such things stayed in there tormenting him perma- nently because this was a man who couldn't bear not understanding every detail — every particle — every crumb of anything that earned his curiosity . . . And I of all people knew how unfriendly his curiosity was . . . How tyrannical . . . like nails being driven into flesh . . . and although I had sympathy for this when I was sane, when I found myself half mad with jealousy and suspicion . . . when doubts would sweep over me like a tidal wave because of little things I picked up here and there — little hints — inklings — then I believed that these obsessions of his . . . those women — his father's murder — his mother's "criminality" as he called it . . . were all too huge . . . too overwhelming . . . too gigantic to ever shed, making his past no past at all . . . making it always now . . . always this minute . . . which was why, when I found myself crazy with doubts I'd become a pair of walking antennae that picked up every little nuance — every tremor — any little scent . . . the way he'd go deadpan and start lighting cigarette after cigarette as he kept swearing up and down *that I was completely out of my mind . . . that those women were all Ancient History — part of the long-dead Past — nothing more than Carcasses!* as he'd shift around, not looking at me as his shoulder started jerking and his eye would get a little nervous twitch as a dumb expression would come over him, like a blank screen had suddenly dropped that I could never penetrate, coupled with an ongoing sympathy for their *"plight"* — "Everybody has to make a living," he'd put it as he'd gaze off into space with a frozen angry look that made me start going frantically through all his trouser pockets when he was sleeping looking for any little scrap of evidence, thinking maybe I'd find a credit card receipt — matches from a hotel, a little pink reminder slip with a phone number on it because like Trixie said, "a wife can always tell — *how could she not!*" . . . and yet wondering the whole time if maybe he was right . . .

maybe I *was* crazy — mad! — completely out of my mind . . . What was wrong with me? as I'd drive over to his office in the middle of the day to see if his car was on the parking lot . . . badger the girl who ran the egg division of World-Wide Poultry, his company now since he bought out Aunt Zelda and Uncle Jack, who was the girl I knew better than I knew the girl who ran the "chickens and feathers" division — call him on his private line over and over to see if he was away from his desk . . . and half the time he was and that would make me frantic! — wild! — as I bounced from blinding rages to the most desolate feelings of despair . . . and in bed . . . faking my heart out even more outrageously . . . even more despicably . . . so terrified was I of losing him.

. . . and then it would pass . . . those mad frenzies of doubt and suspicion . . . as though a ferocious storm, some formidable act of nature, was suddenly over just as suddenly as it had begun as I'd smile as I'd pass the carrots to him at dinner, smiling . . . kiss little Jacob who was the spitting image of him . . . happy . . . feeling the way the beach must feel after the hurricane . . . happy . . . to believe that what he said was true . . . happy . . . that those women and the way they'd stroll and dress and smell with all their secret tricks and ecstasies were really *"ancient history!"* . . . grateful the mistake was mine — that I was crazy like he said . . . grateful those "little flare-ups," so to speak, were *"strictly in my imagination"* . . . glad he wasn't in love with only his own desires anymore . . . but with me — glad that I was his desire . . . glad that he was mine — glad I sprang from that old warm spot in the middle of his armpit where I could always return which was my home — my real home — my only home — my husband, as I'd snuggle close to him . . . relieved that the car that went past every night tooting its horn as it blinked its headlights on and off had nothing to do with him . . . glad the phone that rang at all hours and kept ringing and ringing until I picked the receiver up . . . and when I did . . . as soon as I did . . . whoever it was hung up . . . glad it was a wrong number like he said because I was madly . . . wildly . . . insanely in love with him . . . my husband . . . as I sprang out of bed . . . ran out of the bedroom . . . through the hall . . . through the living room and out onto the terrace stark naked . . . my hair all loose and terrible as I lit a cigarette . . . because I didn't believe him! . . .

. . . not one word that came out of his mouth did I believe!

. . . as I cried out to Trixie to help me . . . to tell me what to do . . . *please!* . . . because I didn't know what to do — what should I do — forget it — confront him . . . say nothing . . . say something . . . tell me *please!* . . . he has someone I was sobbing . . . and I know it . . . only he won't admit it . . . he's lying and I know it . . . and it's not only that he's cheating I was shouting — it's that he's lying about it that makes me crazy — finally it wasn't even the woman so much as the lie — that he lied to me was what I couldn't bear . . . the lie . . . that was driving me insane . . .

. . . as life kept creeping on . . . silently as usual around this giant sinkhole in the middle of our life . . . with breakfast at eight and dinner at seven the same as always — the morning paper folded neatly at his place . . . theater tickets — the movies, dinner with friends on the weekends . . . fresh flowers in big crystal bowls all over the whole apartment, and while Mr. Columbus dozed . . . faint whiffs of gardenia perfume kept rising from the collar of his shirt . . . faint whiffs of gardenia perfume coming from the hairs around his ears . . . his mouth dropped open . . . the evening paper fallen from his hand . . . nothing outwardly any different . . . nothing outward showing . . . except for her — a constant presence now — immutable and real who was always there . . . all the time . . . her gardenia perfume always vaguely every-where . . . the trail of it dotting all the rooms and halls and bathrooms . . . faintly . . . lightly . . . like the dancing end of a beautiful shimmering scarf . . . his dark angel — whom I had to get rid of — of course! . . . only how . . . that was the only question . . .

part five

trying

one

I spotted him at the Wolfe's-Neck Bookstore.

There he was, down in that little basement cave of books — that cramped little madness of books upon books upon more books that were stacked and piled on tables and on the floor and stuffed and packed into all the shelves . . . *Zallow Lustman!* . . . Prizewinning author of maybe the finest horror novels ever written — *THE* Zallow Lustman! . . . as I stopped dead in my tracks — frozen, as a little ecstatic rush of exhilaration came over me, that bizarrely wild excitement of fame — that exploding exhilaration of recognition that makes the person you recognize seem bigger than life — more real than who he really is . . . standing there . . . *THE* Zallow Lustman! . . . as I got my second glimpse of real celebrity — First Rita Hayworth and now Zallow Lustman, as a thrill shot through me that had some shaky little promise attached to it . . . almost a kind of hope . . . as I kept sneaking looks at him in a flip of terror and excitement — which . . . terror . . . or excitement . . . as I began to shake as I kept peeking over the row of books where I was hiding so I could get a better look at that famous face — cheerless, stern, almost ruthless but so gigantically familiar because that face was on the front, not the back, of all his jacket covers under his big red title — his trademark jacket cover — his big mean scowling face glaring at you in every bookstore you walked into so you couldn't miss it — it was so familiar that it was almost like staring at a relative and lately even worse . . . now it was on every magazine cover and in all the bookstore windows and on all the magazine stands everywhere you turned because he had just published his fiftieth horror novel, which won not only every horror book award — every one of them . . . but a Pulitzer as well . . . I knew because I read every book he had ever written because I was a horror book fanatic . . . and Zallow Lustman was in a class completely by himself.

Very pale, which I never dreamed, white as a ghost in fact, and aging, with a narrow pointy face hinting something of the rodent — his little searing eyes like two black coals staring at me over his half-glasses that were perched on his nose like a set of little windshields as I brushed past touching, "sorry," I whispered as I looked down as I was noticing how his thick black eyebrows were crossed and scowling like mean little street-cleaning brushes, the end of the right one flying up like an exotic little wing — his nose a giant sailboat with a thick white edge of hair pulled back into that famous long white ponytail around a bald white shiny head, as he kept staring at me as I purchased a copy of *The Upanishads*, the Penguin Classics edition, and because those beady eyes were still on me . . . probably because he was waiting to see if I was going to pick up one of his books, out of deference to this monumental literary icon I grabbed a copy of *The Shriek*, his latest and then . . . looking down at the floor I waited for my purchases to be rung up, my heart pounding like a small trapped bird was in there trying to get out . . . because I didn't like being stared at . . . it reminded me too much of Nathan Smollens sitting in his leather chair in the darkened living room — no lights, making his leather chair, the living room, and him all that same strange color brown, not saying anything — not a word . . . *nothing!* . . . as I grabbed my yellow paper bag with the books, grabbed my change, and left . . .

It was another scorching August afternoon . . . again so hot there was a heat shimmer all across the park; that strange distortion of shimmering silver waves that seemed to have melted all the marble statues, all the enormous trees and all the great stone benches, rendering them wobbling images within ribbons of wavy silver . . . bending and twisting them, their great knees cracked making them appear to swerve . . . crippled, as though their magnificent collective spirit, their whole noble inanimateness had been broken by the unbearable heat . . . as I walked along, my high heels click click clicking on the hard cement . . . aware that trailing right behind me . . . in all that glaring sunlight . . . *THE Zallow Lustman!*

As I walked faster . . . he walked faster. As I turned up Eighteenth Street he turned up Eighteenth Street — his fierce presence gaining steadily, with an intense, mean feel like a hungry hyena was trailing me — angry almost, in a white shirt — no tie as I kept checking his reflections in all the store windows we were passing. And as I slowly moved away from the buildings to cross the street, so did he — As I crossed Walnut Street he crossed Walnut Street. As I walked faster he walked faster — When I slowed up he slowed up . . . And as I finally came to the light and stopped . . . he came up beside me, still staring at me over the top of his half-glasses . . . as I returned the look, creating that certain click between us finally — that agreement . . . that willingness to go the next step into this game he was challenging me with, framed by a completely flawless sky, blue and gorgeous . . . trees wild with green along the sidewalks, with dazzling sunlight bouncing off the blazing concrete, turning the pavements into fields of sparkling diamonds . . . all of it becoming magical in some fierce and unrelenting way as I began to tremble . . . my limbs becoming heavy — my mouth dry — my heart racing as I was looking directly at this world-famous man . . . almost as famous as Rita Hayworth . . . not knowing what to do — not knowing what to say — and anyhow, who could say anything to *THE Zallow Lustman!* because he wasn't the kind you talk to anyhow, any more than Rita Hayworth was . . . This was someone for whom you automatically become an audience . . . lucky for me because I was one of those people who don't like talking anyhow . . . one of those "selective mutes" as I was tagged in school, who had a life-and-death struggle trying to eke out even a single sound, making the art of conversation a terrible joke . . . my mind didn't know how to do it any more than my mouth or my tongue or my lips or my voice knew how . . . I never discovered the knack . . . and what's more . . . I was married so I had to turn away because even though being married wasn't all that it was cracked up to be . . . and even though Mr. Columbus couldn't be trusted — which of course he couldn't — it was too late for me . . . and anyhow . . . I didn't have the nerve.

. . . and yet . . . if I didn't find the nerve . . . then on my deathbed when it was finally too late, I'd be left with nothing but regrets . . . and worse, my soul which-is-part-of-forever, that part of me that's part of the whole big mystery that never dies can be badly broken from not taking a few little chances here and there because chances are a kind of trust — a kind of faith in life and the spirit knows this, the spirit knows that chances! — daring! — guts! — nerve! and that certain thing called *chutzpah!* are what it's all about — what keeps the spirit thriving . . . but like Mr. Columbus always said, "It takes a lot to put yourself out there" as *THE Zallow Lustman* stood beside me at the light still staring that steady cold-blooded stare, which was the lure that he was casting . . . that I knew that he was casting . . . and yet . . . for some unknowable reason . . . I wanted to get caught on it . . . something like a bear might want to get its foot snared in a trap and be left to die . . .

. . . as Mr. Columbus, that is, the essence of Mr. Columbus . . . his big puffed-up spirit . . . a ghost maybe or something like that . . . in that funny formal suit he wore on our wedding day with that strange white shirt in his shiny new black patent-leather shoes . . . his hair slicked back so far it look like it was painted on . . . his eyes pleading . . .

. . . but it's too late — I'm sorry I whispered, you see, this is my chance now — my turn now I smile to the essence of this man who was begging me not to go . . . reaching out to hold me back — trying to grab on to me with those thick fat penis fingers I tried so hard to love . . . those bizarre fat penis fingers that people were always staring at . . . on trains . . . on buses . . . on airplanes because they were so flagrant — so outrageous and disgraceful that you couldn't take your eyes away . . .

. . . didn't he think I knew what he was up to? — didn't I smell her perfume all over him all the time . . . or see those white satin evening shoes out on our terrace tapping for him to come running in that long white chiffon evening gown with that one thick rhinestone strap going across the other shoulder . . . his dark angel . . . in my house — how dare she? — so yes — what about fidelity — ha! I laugh . . . Faithful to what I scowl at his big puffed-up essence — To whom . . . To a notion —

To an idea that uses my body as the token to the *Myth!*
— *My body Mr. Columbus* which belongs to *Me!* . . . *Not
you* — *Me!* — So Step Aside! . . . because guess what —
*Finally! I AM being faithful only this time it's to ME! . . .
Finally . . . I'm taking back MYSELF* — *which is finally the
only one I should have been faithful to all along* — *to my
dreams* — *to my hopes or else I'm nothing but a Slave!* — *a
Captive!* — *a Vassal! without a self at all which is the worst
travesty of ALL!* I'm whispering as we go through the
revolving doors and into the lush, exquisite lobby of the
Barclay Hotel — me and *THE Zallow Lustman!* . . .

Oh, and before I forget Mr. Columbus . . . ha! ha!
ha! I laugh . . . have you read *The Mummy's Complaint?*
— *The Voice of the Bat?* or *The Mouth?* — Of course
you haven't I sneer at him — because you don't read
books! . . . ha! ha! ha! I'm snickering — as I recall you
only read *The Wall Street Journal* with girlie magazines
inside . . .

Oh, and pardon me Rita Hayworth — before
I forget — have you had a chance to pick up his two
incomparable masterpieces . . . *The Golden Claw* and
Camp Zombie? . . . Both of them marvels of horror and
suspense even if he does have a beak for a nose — huge
yellowish bags under his eyes — a ridiculous long white
ponytail and he's probably a whole foot shorter when
he takes off his gum-soled brown-and-whites . . .

But So What! — Looks aren't Everything! . . .
Genius doesn't have to be attractive does it Nathan

Smollens? — Or even nice, because like he said in *Hello Zombie, "Nice is bullshit — Better to be respected,"* so ha! ha! ha! on you too Nathan Smollens . . . you who made me drab and shabby! — you, Nathan Smollens, who thought I wasn't good enough to ever even *talk to* . . . you who always looked at me with such contempt as if to say that my hair grew up instead of down, my skin was too green . . . my legs were too short — my bust was too big and my eyes too close together and therefore no one would ever *look at me* . . . well, *THE Zallow Lustman* doesn't seem to think so, so ha! ha! ha! on you again as my father . . . still roaming around the house on Twenty-first Street in his yellow satin bathrobe . . . my husband with his pleading eyes and those ten fat penis fingers reaching out to grab me along with her — *his dark angel* . . . *Rita Hayworth* who was still laughing at me under her breath . . . laughing . . . laughing . . . all suddenly vanished . . . puff . . . as we go sailing into the elevator — me and *Zallow Lustman* . . . and for one gleaming moment out of a whole scared and gutless life . . . for one shining instant out of all the boredom and heartache, I was somehow catapulted out of myself and into something that had wings . . . released . . . free . . . sprung loose from all the burdens I never knew I even had . . .

And as the elevator doors closed silently in front of us . . . as the elevator slowly began lighting its way up — up — up — one floor ticking silently past the next all the way up to the penthouse — as we started walking down the long pale hall, his eyes glued to mine as he slipped his arm around my waist . . . I had no past — no pain — no yesterdays, no tomorrows — just a famous genius named *Zallow Lustman* . . . and with him the hope — implicit in his very being . . . of a few exquisite moments of paradise.

two

His hotel room was dazzling white with thick white carpets and shimmering white satin drapes and white satin chairs and sofas all with tufted white satin backs, and long crystal windows floor-to-ceiling gleaming like sparkling ice . . .

It was a whole other world like nothing I had ever seen . . . It even smelled different . . . and still — so still that you could almost imagine seeing a pin falling in slow motion, with something grand and glittering, like a towering wedding cake that promises everything as I stood there staring . . . wonderstruck . . . gazing . . . first at the giant crystal chandelier in the middle of the room, heavy with dangling topaz and amethyst baubles like a piece of colossal jewelry . . .

Old World paintings everywhere in thick gold frames — Night tables that were huge antique dressers with curly brass pulls and thick pink marble tops . . . and between them — the bed . . . terrifying and immense in all its implications . . . waiting . . .

. . . as I gazed at it . . . scared . . . wonderstruck . . . and dazzled . . . not realizing that the whole time I was looking around he was backing me backward over to the door that was still half open as he was pulling up my skirt, while at the same time he was fiddling around with his trousers as he was pulling down my panties . . . and then, when he had me backed up against it — the weight of my body slamming it shut he pulled out his business, fiddled with it a second — slung my leg up onto his arm like he had done it this way so many times that by now this gesture was automatic, a simple one-step operation as he pushed himself against me — jammed it in — threw back his head — made that sound . . . and that was it — done . . . over — finished — as I stood there staring at a topaz and amethyst crystal sconce . . . thinking that cats take longer . . . even dogs . . . as he was pulling up his pants . . .

Don't cry I whispered — Not now . . . as I watched him go into the bathroom, come out a moment later — walk over to the brown leather travel bag that was on the chair, pull out a thick black leather notebook, and still not looking at me I watched him walk over to the bed, sit down with the notebook, take his glasses out of his trouser pocket, put them on, pick up the phone — call room service, and then . . . looking at his thick gold Rolex watch I watched him order a Coke — only one! — then a chicken salad sandwich — only one . . . and as I bent to pick up my panties that were lying crumpled around my foot like a little creature that had been slaughtered, I kept telling myself to just not cry . . . and anyhow . . . cry for what . . . for whom — maybe for what people do to each other without a qualm. . . . maybe for so much courage wasted — or maybe finally for the end of hope —

You're a real winner, kid, he laughed not looking up — some part of him not registering that I was even in the room as he opened his black leather note-book, and still not looking at me made another offhand remark . . . something about being "a first-class sweetie-pie" as though he were someplace else — in another city maybe, or maybe on another planet as he was trying to bridge the awfulness until I was out of there — gone as I jammed the slaughtered little panties into the pocket of my skirt . . . then turned in a move to disappear . . . vanish . . .

What's your name? he laughed still not looking up — Let me guess — Is it Susan or is it Marsha? — Or maybe it's Denise, he quipped still not looking at me as he kept scribbling furiously in the black leather notebook on his lap . . . And by the way, he said still not looking up as he was reaching into his pocket, let me buy you lunch? — Here — Take this, he said as I was standing there begging God to please! — *please! just let me to get out of here alive* as I began to open the door —

Stop! he snapped as he looked up — So what's your name? Tell me, in case I'm ever in this fercockta place again . . .

Don't have one I laughed — Never did, I shouted over my shoulder as I began crying as I was running, running down the long pale hall, tears burning down my face . . . my hand clutching the defiled murdered panties in my pocket . . .

three

Did I regret that I went with him that day — was I mortified . . . were my cheeks burning with humiliation — was I cringing as I realized how hideous the moment was that I allowed myself to be swept into like I was some kind of inhuman instrument — *Yes!* — *Absolutely Yes!* as I kept running, running — my high heels click click clicking across the hard cement . . .

I'm on my way, Mr. Columbus — I'm coming home — Wait for me — Don't go . . . *Please!* — Don't go away, as I pictured Mr. Columbus sleeping on the sofa after dinner, the evening paper fallen from his hand, kindness emanating from his soft warm eyes as he sees me walk in . . . always the big welcoming smile . . . always the goodness — always the gentleness with a touch of something childlike too, something simple and calm . . . he who has given me everything — *everything!* — genuine love — stability — goodheartedness . . . a roof over our heads — a safe haven . . . our precious home, our little son Jacob . . . the intimacy of our bathroom — his towel and my towel next to each other — our soap, his razors — things that make up the quiet joys of life not to mention our kitchen too with everything in it that I had taken so much for granted . . .

But never again — Oh No! . . . Our brooms, our vacuum cleaner . . . our mops and buckets . . . The fake Calder mobile hanging outside the kitchen door that he gave me for my birthday . . . *where I first saw her!* . . .

so how could I call that home! — Home to whom? — to what? . . . to you and Rita Hayworth! . . . Home to the smell of her heavy perfume that was everywhere all the time with her hiding somewhere in the shadows like I didn't see, which means that for me there is no home — I have no home — not anymore . . . as the big puffed-up essence of my husband — the overly inflated core of his whole entire being springs up out of the concrete like a ghost and starts running next to me with a mean accusing look . . . Oh, pardon me Mr. Columbus . . . But how dare *you look at me that way!* — You of all people I snap as I'm wiping my eyes on the back of my hand as we're running past the statue of the lady with the duck . . . Love you? — *Of course* I love you! . . . Yes I loved you when I went off with him — *Of course* I did but loving doesn't necessarily make a person happy — Happiness lies in being **understood** — Not in merely being *Tolerated* and I can't survive anymore the isolation of merely being *Tolerated!* as I suddenly feel our apartment door slam shut with no way back to everything I need and cherish . . . my home — my husband, my brooms and mops and curtains and rugs and lamps — to all my belongings — *to everything I have* as my high-heeled shoes keep click click clicking across the hard concrete sounding almost like the tick tick of a clock . . . almost like the sound of time running out . . . oh, you're a tough one Solomon Columbus I laugh as terror begins in little choking gasps . . . only terror of what — The terror of being found out! — Caught! . . . as I try to fake another little laugh, some little cajoling gesture to placate him as we're running past the birdbath . . . Oh, you mean Zallow Lustman? ha! ha! ha! — what about him I laugh again pretending to be amused by the silliness of the question . . . what do you mean? . . . not that old nonsensical unwritten law that says that it's okay for you but not for me I keep laughing . . . *oh please!* — not that old ridiculous dim-witted view that says that the whole wide world and everything in it is yours because you're a *man,* but if I try for even one little moment's worth of happiness I'm a *slut*! — a no-good dirty piece of filthy *trash*! well no thanks I laugh, because the definition of *"slut* and a no-good dirty piece of filthy *trash"* is to do harm to a fellow creature so what you don't know can't do you any harm and anyhow, what did I take away from you by having a moment with someone else — *Nothing!* — *Absolutely Nothing* I begin shouting as we're running past the blue-tile pond . . . only running where? — where am I running as his ten fat penis fingers start reaching out . . . again . . . trying to grab on to me . . . again . . . because nothing stops him! — *nothing!* — not this dark swarthy sex monster with his deep calm insatiable lust that neither unfaithfulness, insults, nor being spit at — cursed or slapped across the face or kicked even fazes when he's after what he wants . . . as he's trying . . . *trying* to grab my arm as we're tearing past the statue of the goat as I'm clutching the defiled, humiliated pair of murdered panties in the pocket of my skirt — my lipstick smeared — thick streaks of black mascara streaming down my face like the tears of a clown . . . You Solomon Columbus with no chinks in the armor — ha! I shout as I'm trying to wipe my nose on the shoulder of my blouse — *look who has the nerve to talk about Betrayal!* — *You who've betrayed me left and right . . . All the time! . . .* Oh, don't deny it *please* ha! I shout again, only now I'm shouting really loud as I'm wiping my eyes on my arm as I'm running, running . . . *Yes, that's exactly what I said* — *Betrayed me left and right* — *All the time!* — If I kick you under the table in a private gesture to tell you to shut up in front of people because you're saying something I don't want anyone to hear and you say "what did you kick me for?" — that's a *betrayal!* — In Atlantic City when you told me in front of your aunt and uncle to "stop feeling sorry for myself," when I had every right in the world to feel sorry for myself — that's being *betrayed* Solomon Columbus I'm shouting as we're running past the crouching lion in the flower bed . . .

But that wasn't the worst of it Solomon Columbus, any more than Rita Hayworth was the worst of it and whoever else you lied to me about — The worst Solomon Columbus, was when you betrayed ENIAC which was when you betrayed *Yourself* for a closet full of Gucci belts back when money became your whole entire story — your *"God in circulation"* as you put it . . . back when you first bought into being *rich*! . . . But not me oh no . . . not me Solomon Columbus I'm shouting . . . no . . . I swaggered out and took my chance with a Zallow Lustman — yes! . . . okay! . . . I'll tell you if you want to know, Zallow Lustman was my stab at hope I'm sobbing . . . my stab at the dream . . . at freedom . . . my stab at finally being *real* — Zallow Lustman was that simple hunger for one's own self and the need to assert that self without apology to you or to anyone, and even if that self has been crushed and broken into a thousand little pieces it's still me in there Mr. Columbus, and what I do is up to me — *me!* . . . as I clutched my defiled humiliated panties even more tightly as I was running running through the fading afternoon on what seemed then the worst day of my life, because it was the assumption then of abject failure — complete and absolute . . . But that was because I didn't know then that success teaches nothing — like I didn't know then that the source of all the richness of spirit . . . all that's magnificent in all its contradictory truths . . . all that's genuine and powerful that understands beyond all understanding comes from all the terrible failures that have scorched and honed and molded us into who we'll finally be . . . only I didn't know this then so I didn't value then the courage it took to take a chance with a Zallow Lustman, same as I didn't know then that failure has nothing to do with rejection, or with humiliation, or with losing; it has only to do with not fighting back.

part six

Trixie

Part 3.8

Trixie

one

Every Thursday, from the very first days of my marriage I had lunch with Trixie . . . always hopeful . . . always optimistic that something good would come, and now I was even more hopeful — even more optimistic that this time she'd come through for me because no matter what he said, no matter how he swore up and down, no matter how many Bibles he put his hand on I was convinced it was still going on full-force . . . him and Rita Hayworth.

Usually I would arrive at her apartment shortly before noon, the apartment she moved into after she finally sold the old red-brick Federal on Twenty-first Street that contained all the remains of Nathan Smollens . . . his clothes, his smells and his ghost that was still roaming around somewhere on the second floor in his yellow satin bathrobe, which was maybe why she had to move — to get away from him — because maybe she knew . . . like I know now, that the dead don't die — it isn't that easy.

The "new house," or so she called it even though it wasn't a house; it was a small apartment that was part of an assisted-living complex on the square, and it wasn't new; she had been living for the past three years in this cramped little space that was formerly an office building, so it had a dreary office building quality, but it was still up the social ladder — Trixie was finally on Rittenhouse Square — her lifelong dream — the same square where I played as a child, walked through every day on my way to school, and where a man named Solomon Columbus sat down beside me on a bench one roasting August afternoon and offered me a cigarette . . .

Rittenhouse Square — For her the swanky pinnacle of where to be . . . for me, the lush green blossoming core of the whole ancient umbilicus — the most outside part of the deepest connection, a place that no matter how far I'd move in any direction it would always be my own personal North Star — my own private nexus, where long ago she pushed a carriage with me inside . . .

Her "new house," like our old one that always smelled funny smelled funny too . . . It was that stale, sweet old-lady smell, something arid with a hint of camphor with her belongings (or what was left of them) somehow off — somehow all out of kilter like messy hair . . . Her chairs and lamps and little knickknacks were like displaced persons, somehow rootless and floating even though she had been living there for the past three years . . . Cartons were still unpacked in the corners of the rooms . . . mirrors on the floor that were never hung . . . pictures stacked up against the wall . . . something transient, shabby with her sitting in her tattered old red velvet throne beside the window, waiting . . . how long I wondered as I walked in, would she be sitting in that same red velvet chair waiting for me . . . how long I wondered . . . would she call every morning to tell me to stay home that day because it was "too cold to go outside" . . . or because "it was raining that day" . . . or because that day "the sun was too bright," which meant that I should stay in or I'd go blind if I dared look up — worry, terror, and fear were how she loved . . .

"Out of sight, out of mind," she sighed her usual languid indolent greeting, slow and tortured as she turned up her face as though she were bestowing an honor . . . And as I bent to kiss her bony cheek that was permanently slippery from all the years of Pond's Cold Cream that had been patted into it so religiously, I too became slippery . . . "Your hair's a mess!" she sighed wearily as she gazed languorously at me as though she was finally running out of the steam it took to give an honest insult, her eyes scanning me scornfully from the two big pink half-moons circling them like thumbprints, with a big sharp beak, long thin white hair like feathers, and a face so deeply lined that it looked as if some violent creature had taken a chisel and carved maliciously into even her, Trixie Smollens, who had waged such a ferocious war to become immune to all the devastations — Trixie Smollens, who had waged such a ferocious battle against Time . . . "How many times do I have to tell you to let your hair *alone* — but no," she sighed, "you have to keep coloring it and chopping it — Can't stand looking good can you?" she scoffed as she looked away contemptuously.

"Hi Trixie," I countered very carefully because the inclination was to forget who I was dealing with . . . to lose sight of the fact that not only was she a valiant worrier, she was also mean-spirited, shrewd, and fey making her extremely dangerous . . . and since I needed counseling on the subject of Rita Hayworth . . . I had to be extra careful because of my current neediness, not to let down my guard . . . not even for a minute . . . or she'd eat me whole . . .

. . . and what's more — much more . . . I had to follow certain very rigorous rules — The first was that I could never dare ask her how she was or how she was doing, or how she was feeling because that would instantly enrage her — "ah, just waiting for me to die is she? . . . just waiting for me to get sick and pass away so she can get her hands on all my belongings . . . on all my knick-knacks and trinkets and bric-a-brac and lamps and on all my exquisite rings and bracelets and earrings, huh? — Well, not so fast!" she'd smolder if I dared even broach the subject so I never asked — The rules were clear, I was strictly limited to saying either "Hi" or "Hello" and then shutting up — That's how the first round of our visits had to begin.

"You'll find out," she'd begin as she began pulling herself slowly up out of the chair, "that the one thing in life that ruins everything isn't poverty, or illness or even the prospect of death — *It's Boredom!* and the older you get the more boring it all becomes, until finally even your own name will begin to bore you if you live long enough," she'd glare at me with contempt . . . (or maybe it was rage) as she launched herself slowly out of her chair and started walking slowly toward the closet in the hall . . . her remarkable posture — strong and straight as a ramrod once the transition from sitting to standing had been accomplished and she was all the way up . . .

Extremely short, not quite five feet, making her look like a staunch little penguin — stiff, straight, and powerful with that great battle stride that she flashed against death every minute of her life . . . her biggish feet in sheer black stockings that each had two little holes . . . no runs, just two little holes per stocking, with her black suede shoes that had thick ridged soles and her long slow loping stride . . . something emanating from the perspective of survival — some trick she must have picked up somewhere about not tripping, each great loping step covering a vast amount of territory with her eyes looking straight ahead, not down as if she were blind . . . "It used to be nonstop fun all the time — what a blast!" she continued as she stopped in front of the closet in the hall to yank out her big red cape . . . (a cape I wouldn't mind having myself I was thinking as I watched her fling it around her shoulders like a retired matador) — sling her pocketbook across the other shoulder so it hung directly in front of her belly button as she turned away from the closet and began walking fiercely forward — her feet feeling their way as they went like little mountain goats . . . "but I can't complain," she said, "I was young and beautiful and as fresh as springtime until just last week . . . radiant, alive, and vital — I walked like a dancer — had the strength of a prizefighter and wore nothing but gorgeous bracelets and earrings every single day of my life — it didn't matter, silver, plastic, or even gold sometimes, and for a long time gorgeous ankle bracelets too, 'all the precious ammunition' as Balzac put it," she said as she looked at me with an odd quizzical look as though it were I, not she who had just said something she didn't understand . . . these strange little twists of hers . . . bizarre and mysterious always popping up as I nodded in agreement to who-knows-what . . . as I was wondering as I was looking at her how old she was . . . I didn't know — I never knew . . . all I knew was that she was a lot older than I . . . much older, old enough to be my grandmother because once when she was loaded she glared at me and said that she was too old to have ever had a child — then something about her "change-of-life baby" as she kept glaring at me . . . Once one of my aunts, her sister Sylvia who ate only in the dark, had eleven cats, and whom everyone called "Tuss" because of her enormous ass, told me vis-à-vis that she was almost fifty when I was born and once her brother Monroe who wore a silver breastplate hanging from a chain around his neck so that he looked like a walking Torah told me that she was fifty-one when I was born but if I ever dared ask she'd accuse me of trying to put a curse on her . . . Age was one of her terrible subjects, so I always backed off — I never opened my mouth, not willing to lose her on a technicality as I watched her slam the door of her apartment and then vigorously jiggle the knob to make sure it was locked as I stood there wondering how many more afternoons like this . . . how much longer — because everything bounces off death — everything . . . my mother . . .

"But it got too hard to get those goddamn ankle bracelets on and off," she went on, "and truthfully? . . . why wear ankle bracelets anyhow . . . by now I've outlived most of them, at least all the interesting ones," she sighed with a hint of weary triumph as she went back to looking straight ahead as she was speaking as though I weren't there — as though no one were, and as we were getting into the elevator she continued philosophizing with herself because for her there was never anyone there, because for her no one existed on the face of the entire planet except Beatrice Greenburg Smollens — Goddess! which was maybe why she had that permanently blank faraway look . . . because she wasn't curious about anything and nor did she care about anything either as she pressed the *down* button twice —

"After all," she smiled, still staring straight ahead, "as I've said — all the interesting ones are gone and the rest of them are hardly worth the effort — Yesterday Rosa told me to greet that boring Mr. and Mrs. Marcus who were standing in the lobby grinning at me," she went on, "but I flatly refused . . . I simply wasn't in the mood — I didn't feel like greeting that Mrs. Marcus one more time.

In the first place she's the biggest phony that ever walked the earth — Cold, calculating, driven socially, and *Cheap*! — And as for him with his big capped teeth — why must I say hello?" she asked as she looked straight at me with that odd, quizzical look again, like it was I who had just said something she didn't understand — that same odd peculiarness of hers as the elevator doors closed us in and then began its slow descent . . . the floors ticking their way down . . . down . . . carrying the two of us like two little kernels, each encased in our own little crystal balls, the crystals touching sometimes — sometimes not — the kernels never because it isn't possible — that urge for unity . . . that overwhelming drive for oneness — for completion that can never happen — *"Birth, the wound that never heals"* . . . who said that I was wondering as I was half looking — half gazing at her in a kind of stupor . . . my mother . . . who was smiling to herself as she was gazing at the elevator ceiling . . . "Once — and not so long ago," she was musing wistfully, "life was crackling with excitement and anticipation — every minute a Triumph," she sighed as she began blowing her nose into a rumpled Kleenex . . . "Not so long ago — believe it or not, I was young and radiant," she sighed as she looked at me as the elevator doors opened and we started walking . . . her astonishingly firm posture like a robust little penguin . . . her feet moving like they were schooled in knowing exactly how not to trip almost like they had eyes . . . Survival — the whole story for Trixie Smollens . . . as she took my hand.

two

The Rittenhouse Restaurant was our usual spot — The greenish light in there . . . the high ceilings, the long Victorian bar — the army of little mahogany tables and chairs, the elegant gloominess of that bustling building on the square that was always jumping, always crowded and packed as though people were happy to bear the wait — lines of people . . . to get their egg-salad-and-pimento sandwich, their frozen chocolate dessert with the heavy marshmallow topping, and the homemade fudge sold by the pound in big glass counters near the door.

"So, shall we have our usual?" she asked.

"Yes," I answered . . . Business first. That was Trixie which was good, because it gave me a chance while she was ordering to decide if I should divulge my devastation concerning Rita Hayworth knowing on the one hand that I should keep my mouth shut of course . . . except the temptation to seek her advice was overwhelming . . . always . . . why this was so I can't say because in the first place she never gave good advice . . . In fact, she always gave insane advice like . . . "if it isn't fun don't do it," or . . . "if you hear bad news, immediately walk out the nearest door backward" . . .

And second, it was leaving myself wide open because she'd start asking a million questions that were none of her business — intruding herself — interfering — bad-mouthing Mr. Columbus because according to her he was "a greasy slob who came from a vile background — Sephardic Jews — Ich!" she would say and then she'd start criticizing me for everything wrong I ever did in my whole entire life, which she would claim was what led to this disaster, which she would also claim she could have predicted, blah blah blah . . .

"So how's the slimy grease-ball?" she'd sneer . . . (mean as usual — nasty . . . biting) — But still . . . there was always the hope — always the prayer that under that nasty veneer there beat a loving welcoming heart, so there was always the hope that the next time — always the next time — there would be a genuinely loving outpouring — one day . . . sooner or later . . . if not today then the next time if I only had a little more patience — just a little she'd smile at me and put her hand on mine as a great loving force would come flying out of her . . .

"Fine," I answered . . . hoping against hope on the one hand that this would be the day . . . and on the other . . . hoping that I'd have the strength to just shut up and not say anything if this wasn't the day no matter how much I craved confiding things in her . . . telling her things . . . sharing . . . only why — why did I crave confiding in her — she was mean spirited and nasty and never gave good advice — didn't I know this, so what was the lure . . . as we sat there . . . two little kernels again — each sitting completely encased in our own little crystal ball across from each other with nothing touching . . . not in any way . . . not even the crystals . . .

as we gazed at each other awkwardly . . . looking for something . . . each of us . . . only what . . . as the craving to tell her what was going on with Mr. Columbus began gaining . . . gaining . . . the craving to divulge . . . to wipe away the dividing line between her and me in a desperate effort to erase the inexorable aloneness . . . dissolve the irreversible separateness . . . the crushing urge to inhale Trixie into me or be inhaled by her that could never happen . . . not with her or with anyone — not ever . . . which was what was so terrible . . . we're born alone — we live alone . . . we die alone and when we're dead . . . the horror of being even more alone — completely alone . . . forever!

"I'm speaking to you! — What are you? — *Deaf?* . . . I'm asking you a question!"

"What?" I asked as I looked at her . . . she . . . who gave me death the same as she gave me life so that a sense of mourning was always moving between us in big wild waves . . . the unending sorrow of looking at your mother . . . the child who has to grow up and leave . . . the mother who has to grow old and die . . . she . . . who engenders such thoughts just by gazing at me with that thick dark eye encircled in that big pink thumbprint . . . because she made me . . . and in making me I became part of the whole long living chain that would one day snap . . . and that's what she gave me too . . . an endless universe of death . . . my own . . . hers and everyone's and everything's . . . every plant and every flower . . . every dream and every hope . . . but I could never mention this — oh no! not so much as a hint . . . I had to be forever grateful and my gratitude had to be as big and as absolute and as perfect as death itself . . . *"Do you hear me?"* she was shouting — *"I'm asking how that grease-ball is?"*

"Fine," I answered, tottering just on the edge . . . tottering . . . just on the brink of letting her in . . . with no way out — a door would slam and that would be that, which would be a big mistake and I knew it . . . didn't I know by now that nothing would make her happier than to know that there was a little trouble brewing . . . didn't I know by now that nothing would give her more pleasure than a little misfortune . . . not a big misfortune — no, nothing like that — a big misfortune would simply make her lose interest . . . but a lesser, little misfortune, like my husband running around with Rita Hayworth — This would be *Exhilarating* — *Magnificent!* — *Pure Manna* . . . so why not tell her — why not give her this gift because after all, didn't I have every right to give her anything I wanted and that way ensure a permanent closeness — bind her to me once and for all . . . guarantee it . . . she and I — the two of us . . . forever . . . so why not . . . why not turn to her — after all, didn't I have that right . . . no! because she gave me death the same as she gave me life for one thing . . . don't forget that — don't forget that whole dark other side — the crushing, destroying — withholding side of who she is . . . and what's more . . . it would never bind her to me in a closeness where there would be a real outpouring of loving kindness and genuine sympathy — To the contrary! She would have complete contempt for me for having let such a thing happen in the first place . . . Trixie loved winners not losers, and furthermore, the knowledge of it would turn her into a warring animal that would turn on me with everything she had . . . It would give her the right to ask a million new unheard-of questions that were none of her business — Violate every boundary and start wildly swatting at anyone I cared about whom I'd then have to defend . . . like my husband whom she detested because maybe I loved him more than I loved her . . . or all my friends — every one of them whom I loved which she couldn't stand . . . and worst of all . . . my little son Jacob because I was wild about him and she knew it . . . why these objections I can't say exactly except to say that not only did she need to be the only one — *period!* — she had a constantly lurking melancholy that threw off a strangeness in her that showed itself as an aversion to anything natural and normal — even you might to say anything *good* — anything *decent* — she hated that . . . Trixie lived in her own little world that I could never enter . . . No one could so that it was finally more like dancing with her than living with her and even though I knew all the steps and could maneuver very carefully around all the pitfalls like a small ship darting in and out around gigantic icebergs, I never understood the music we were dancing to . . . not ever . . . because there were too many mysteries — too many untruths, too much not knowing what was real and what was crazy . . . All I could do was be careful not to hope too much . . . Not to dream too much that one day she might come out of it long enough to reach over, put her hand on mine, and smile — that was all — nothing else — no words . . . just for her to reach over one day, put her hand on mine and smile, which was the dream that kept bringing me back Thursday after Thursday — every Thursday — year in and year out as I watched her rummaging around in her pocketbook looking for a Kleenex . . . "I said — how's the grease-ball — *Sephardic Jews! Ich!*" she said . . . more quietly this time — more suspiciously . . . suddenly eyeing me . . . keen as a hungry sewer rat . . . something was up and she knew it as she began blowing her nose . . . wily as ever . . . so why not tell her — why not just come out with it and give her one last chance to come through . . . maybe now that she's getting up there, maybe she doesn't have much spit and venom left so maybe it's only fair to give her this one last opportunity because after all she was my mother so it would be completely natural and normal to turn to her . . . because after all . . . who else is there on the entire planet who's supposed to care which was how I justified the pitiful hope — the pathetic longing I harbored still . . .

"Well, to be honest," I said as I cleared my throat,

"there just so happens to be a problem — My heart is broken," I murmured as I looked at her.

"What's wrong!" she gasped as she soared out of her miasma, all ears as she glared at me, suddenly perking up at the hint of a little action as I see her readying herself — a stony look, something within her hardening across her face as she leaned toward me . . .

"Mr. Columbus has someone," I said as I gazed at her . . . sheepishly, a sense of failure instantly beginning . . . Instant regret and remorse mushrooming for needing something from her — *anything!* which I was trying to buy by telling her a secret — a kind of tit-for-tat you could say — I'll confide in you if you'll show a little love and kindness, a little sympathy — *pathetic!* . . . *"The only thing worse than the tyrant is the tyrant's victim"* — *Right!* . . . as I was trying to barter for love — barter for compassion, which was like trying to buy the love of the lady in the portrait above the fireplace whom I could never reach or touch or smell and I knew it like I knew it was a big mistake to have opened my mouth in the first place, but it was too late . . . I failed . . . again . . .

"No!" she gasped as she leaned closer so she could hear me better . . . "Believe me — He has no one," she volleyed instantly. "Who in her right mind would look at that slimy dark-complected *grease-ball*? — *Ich!*" she said — "So dark! — So oily! — *So Sephardic — Ich!* — And those *fingers!* — *Ich!* . . . And that fake tan of his — Where does he come off to a year-round tan like that, with all that greasy hair slicked back like a rumba dancer or some kind of Spic band leader from Puerto Rico . . . But you love him, don't you?"

"Yes," I said, quietly.

"Poor you," she said flatly as she looked away contemptuously.

"Why poor me?"

"Because it's a great mistake to love," she said as she kept looking contemptuously off into space . . .

"A mistake *to love* . . . ?"

"Yes," she glared as she looked back at me furiously . . . "Stay to yourself — Depend on no one — Get used to being alone — Don't love anyone *and never be sociable* — otherwise you come in contact with *People!* — You develop attachments to *People!* — All those selfish disgusting nauseating *Jerks* out there who are only out for themselves —

"Believe me," she said solemnly, "they're only hanging around to see what they can get from you — Take my word, that's all you mean to them — Whatever it is *They* need," she said as she glared at me . . . "But No! — You never listen to me do you — You have to do it your way don't you, which I can assure you is exactly the *wrong* way to do *everything!*" she glared as she looked contemptuously off into space again — Fury! her one-size-fits-all response to everything . . . Bad news — Good news — Tragedy, Disaster, Joy — Terror — Pain . . . All of them instantly and equally enraging as the waitress, a little black wiry bird, skinny as a toothpick with long fuchsia fingernails like the humped shells of a school of exotic little sea beasts, was putting down her egg-salad-and-pimento sandwich, her Pepsi . . . and next to it her glass of extra ice.

"Your father might have once had someone," she mused as she began gazing dreamily into space — "Maybe? — I was never absolutely sure," she said as she took a sip of her Pepsi — "Sometimes he used to come home late from the office in very high spirits — a little too high for my two cents — It was always on those Thursday nights when he said he had 'a few particularly hard extractions,' and that's when I'd catch him humming and whistling as he'd salute himself in the mirror in the hall like he was in the army . . . *as Nathan Smollens suddenly flashed by . . . thick and blown up like a giant English bulldog with his big potbelly . . . his thick shoulders hunched over from peering too long into too many people's mouths . . . his presence still enormous . . . glaring at me in his yellow satin robe — death did nothing to help . . . nothing . . .*

"Like I've always said," she smirked as she took a bite of her egg-salad-and-pimento sandwich, "the strange thing about human beings is that the better you are to them the more they crap on you — But you don't believe me about that either — No!" she said, her eyes set deep inside those big pink thumbprints, glaring — "How many times have I told you to throw in a little *Disdain!* — A little *Contempt!*" she said as she took another infuriated bite — "There's an old Jewish saying," she said, her mouth stuffed, packed and bulging with rye bread, egg salad, and pimentos — *"Disregard to get Regard!* — In the first place he would like you better that way — Much better! And in the second, it would keep him jumping so he could never get too comfortable . . . But you can't do this can you because you're *Afraid* of him — Isn't that so? . . . I think you're too afraid of him to employ even a few very simple tactics," she said as she glared at me . . . "But tell me . . . Why? — Why are you afraid of that dark oily *Jerk* — *Ich*!" she said as she glared off into space again, outraged — "He's so ugly — *Ich*!" she sneered — "So dark and oily like he was dipped in *Grease*! — but never mind — You're afraid of something — of losing him or something — something like that — Isn't that so?"

"Yes," I answered . . . annoyed . . . because as pushy and as nasty as she was, she was as equally canny and this infuriated me . . .

"So tell me, why are you afraid of losing *him*?" she asked as she stared at me incredulously . . .

"Because I love him," I answered.

"You love *Him*?" she said . . . like I was talking about a two-headed baboon whom she had never encountered and therefore couldn't fit, no matter how hard she tried, into what we were talking about — she simply didn't get it as she kept staring at me — "Are you saying that you're afraid of *Him because you Love him*?" she asked — completely baffled . . .

"Human misery is revealed in all its nakedness in connec-

tion to love," I answered, quoting Simone Weil . . .

"No! — That's not the reason!" not the least bit interested in Simone Weil, whom she probably never read because she claimed she hated Jewish writers . . .

"You're afraid of losing him because you were *terrified* of your father! — That's why . . . But tell me — why were you so afraid of Nathan Smollens? — That's what I'd like to know — Maybe because you're one of those people who don't know the difference between love and *hate!*" she snapped . . . *"Indifference is the opposite of love! — Not hate!* and your father was *anything but indifferent to you! — Anything!"* she glared at me — *"My God — how that man loved you!* — Maybe a little too much if you know what I mean — Maybe a little too 'Freudian' if you know what I'm saying — Maybe he was *in love with you* — It happens," she said . . . "But since love brings out the worst in everyone . . . and maybe because you were so young, maybe you didn't understand the way this love affected him — Maybe," she said as she looked at me — "you didn't understand that it even *was* love. But I can tell you this," she said as she peered straight into me, "your father loved you — I would even say *too much!*" she said as she kept glaring at me — her one good eye staring into mine with those big pink thumbprints all around them both like big pink nets that could slip over me to catch all my terrors as my terrors tried to scamper like little mice . . . I was still scared of her . . . scared to death . . . "Come on!" I fake-laughed in a feeble effort to shut her up . . . in a pathetic attempt to stop her from bringing up the subject of Nathan Smollens which was like waving a red flag as I kept fake-laughing because I didn't want to talk about him and she knew it — it was a terrible subject and she knew it so I just started laughing . . . I just sat there and started faking it again like I faked it all the time with Mr. Columbus, only this time it was a fake ha! ha! ha! — oh boy! that's a good one Trixie — ha! ha! ha! instead of moaning and screaming or instead of telling her straight out that she didn't have a clue — that she didn't know what she's talking about and probably never did because she's probably out of her mind and probably always was . . . as it begins to dawn on me . . . that maybe the time has come to start telling her the truth — to start being straight with her . . . to start getting a little courage going . . . a little gumption . . . a little guts and nerve which a person isn't born with . . . it's something she has to earn — acquire . . . something she has to fight toward . . . *as a voice — something emanating from way down deep began whispering . . . okay Ramona! — the time has come to start telling the truth . . . and telling it all the time . . . and telling it with the most animal-like simplicity . . . because if you can't have her love, which maybe you never can . . . you'll at least be real — no more lies . . . and you'll find that's exhilarating . . .*

"I'm asking you a question — Why were you so afraid of your father?"

———

"To answer your question," I began, my hands beginning to shake because the time had come — no more lies as I cleared my throat . . . "I was afraid of my father because there was something dark in him . . . something disconnected — he wasn't normal," I said as I looked dead at her — "He never spoke to me . . . He never smiled at me — He hardly ever looked at me," I said in a frail scared voice — thin, like a sheet of ice . . . "which made me terrified of him . . ."

. . . that's right . . . good girl . . . keep it up . . . just tell the truth and tell it with the most animal-like simplicity . . . that's all you have to do Ramona it was whispering whispering . . . whispering . . . and even if you'll never have her love because maybe you never will . . . you'll at least be real . . . no more lies and you'll find that's very exhilarating . . .

"When he'd come in at night," I said, my hands still shaking as I cleared my throat again, "I could feel the rage in him — the tautness of it like an arrow poised at me so I'd instantly become on guard because in only a matter of seconds he'd become a rabid animal — a wild dog or a raving hyena — the instant he saw me something awful would come over him even though I did nothing — said nothing, I wouldn't dare . . . which meant that I lived in terror . . . I lived in torture . . . I lived in constant punishment — I lived in a sense of worthlessness all the time . . . and if sometimes he'd spin around and glare at me that glare became like a scar that was burned into me that I could never shake, leaving me with a terrible sense of homesickness even though I was home — and do you know what that means?" I asked the woman sitting across from me who was smirking now — amused . . . "It means that for me there was no home . . . It means that for me there could never be a home . . . I had no home because I was afraid of him and when you're afraid of your father you're afraid of everyone so you never have a home," I said as I leaned toward her so that our faces were almost touching . . .

"And what's even worse," I said . . . "you did nothing — You could have helped me but you didn't . . . You just looked the other way," I whispered as I stared at her . . .

"Let's get back to your husband," she said in a hurry to change the subject . . . "You're absolutely sure he has someone?"

"Yes," I said . . . Stunned . . . by the thrill of finally speaking up . . . Stunned . . . by the exhilaration of finally telling the truth, and telling it with the most animal-like simplicity . . .

"How do you know?" she asked, fake interest springing into her face as though she were suddenly fascinated, which was the trick she always used to change the subject —

. . . never mind her tricks . . . just keep going it was

whispering . . . the little voice of my soul that was pushing for courage, truth — rebirth — a little guts, a little
chutzpah . . . go on Ramona it said . . . keep telling her
the truth and tell it with the most animal-like simplicity,
that's all you have to do it was whispering . . . whispering . . . because even if you'll never have her love —
you'll at least be real — no more lies . . . and you'll find
that's *very* exhilarating . . .

"I'm asking you . . . how do you know he has
someone?"

"In the first place he reeks from perfume all the
time," I answered flying with excitement now, into this
new bright place where there were no more lies, no
more secrets . . . no more silences and darkness . . . this
whole bright new gleaming world where everything was
clear and clean . . . "You can smell it on him the minute
he walks in the door," I said. "And second, the phone
rings at all hours of the night and as soon as I pick the
receiver up . . . every time . . . whoever it is hangs up . . .
every single time! . . . and on top of that," I said, still flying
on my first real stab at being myself — my first real stab
at being real — my first real stab at *authenticity! which is
Everything!* . . . "every night a car goes through the alley
in the back of our building and toots as it blinks its headlights on and off," I said as I looked at her . . . as though
her face, without speaking — without saying a word
would silently confirm these fears and tell me just by
looking at me that she validated me absolutely . . . her

face, just by looking at me, would tell me that I wasn't imagining this . . . that I wasn't crazy, which is even worse than being right . . .

"So? — The car could be for someone who lives across the street," she finally said — "The perfume I don't know about, it could be some cheap Sephardic hair tonic . . . and as for the phone," she said, amused by my suspicions — "it could simply be a wrong number — or . . . knowing his family," she said — "that awful aunt and uncle in Atlantic City and all his other gangster relatives, your phone is probably tapped."

"What's that supposed to mean?" I asked as I looked straight at her, still riding the crest of my new ability to speak the truth . . . still strengthened by this new morality that said that the luxury of honesty was finally mine — and knowing too that no matter how late I was finding it . . . it was like finally finding daylight.

"Those shady partners of his in the chicken-and-egg business — *please!*" she said — "that despicable aunt and uncle in Atlantic City and his father and his mother too — Crooks, All of them — All those gamblers and gangsters and hookers — *please* — you don't think for one minute that his father was shot during a *robbery do you?*"

"*Of course* I think his father was shot during a robbery," I answered, infuriated.

"Well I don't and I never did," she smiled as she gazed dreamily off into space — "That was no robbery

— That was *a 'hit'!* Probably a gambling debt," she smirked as she took a sip of her Pepsi and then went back to gazing dreamily off into space . . . "You married into the lowest bunch of gangsters, gamblers, murderers, hit men, pimps, and prostitutes — or in other words *'the Mob,'*" she sneered — *"'The Mob!'"* she said again as she glared at me . . . "But did I ever once mention this? — No!" she snapped as she kept glaring at me, finally completely out of her miasma and as keen again as a hungry rat — "And why? Because I know how to keep my mouth shut," she snapped — "I know how to preserve my strength and beauty by not passing on ugly thoughts and ugly information because passing on ugly thoughts and ugly information makes *you Ugly!* — It makes your *skin dry!* — It gives *you big ugly pimples* and a *fat backside* so I always make it a point to forget what's ugly and remember only what glows in the dark from its own exquisite inner *Essence* . . . So — does that answer your ridiculous question about him having another woman? — Could anyone *possibly* have another woman if my suspicions are correct?"

"Of course!" I answered as I glared at her . . .

"Oh for God's *sake!* — Then in that case," she shot back as she glared back at me for a long and hostile moment . . . "there's *always* 'another woman' . . . and if there isn't . . . you'd invent one."

"This one is real," I said as I flashed a smug little

victory smile — A little curled half sneer that was glowing with courage and immense self-respect because I was finally fighting back all right . . . finally . . . and so ferociously that I might even win this round . . .

. . . but I was flashing my victory smile too soon . . . sneering at her prematurely . . . because the whole time she had been stalking me like one of those great animals of prey that registers every crumb . . . every nuance . . . every expression on my face . . . nothing escaped her . . . nothing — so now . . . like a big cat crouching in the high grass . . . now . . . waiting for exactly the right moment because I was celebrating and she knew it because she was smart like she knew I was praying that everything fake and awful in my life was finally over . . . praying I would never have to go back to lying . . . not to her or to anyone . . . ever . . . as she glared at me with the appetite of the hungry beast that has waited long enough . . . now . . . she figured she better pounce with a question or two that was none of her business — violate a few boundaries in a hurry . . . disregard all the laws of tact and decency, which was her specialty, or else she might lose the battle for supremacy — *god forbid!* because if she did — *I might finally stand on my own two feet and break free!* . . . as she took a slow calculated bite of her sandwich . . . took a sip of her Pepsi — chewed for a minute . . . and then . . . not looking at me as she cleared her throat she said, "Okay big shot — if you're so sure . . . who is she — what's her name?"

. . . as the Rittenhouse Restaurant came tumbling down softly as I felt the earth crack open as I began sinking . . . sinking . . . because now of course I had to lie because she went too far . . . as I began drowning in that same old gutless place again where there is no courage — no fight . . . no truth . . . which means she won this round by asking a question that was none of her business . . . by going much much farther than I invited her . . . by trespassing all my boundaries — so she won because I didn't know how to answer — I didn't know how to give what I wanted to give and keep what belonged to me — not yet — it was all too new, this business of telling the truth . . .

. . . Today life changed because today for the first time I was real — I told the truth and I told it with simplicity and courage — but handling a direct question aimed at me like a bullet — there I didn't stand a chance because there she knew how to ask for anything! — violate any boundary! — cross any line! — invade anyone's privacy without losing a beat because she, Trixie Smollens — *was the queen of trespassing* . . . and at the top of that fiendish mountain . . . at the very pinnacle . . . at the summit of all transgressions was daring — *daring!* to ask for *a name!* . . . because asking for a *name! is never done!* — *names are off limits!* . . . *and she knows this!* . . . She *knows* that *names* are too big . . . too unspeakable — *names!* — those monster things that are too private and too sinister because they reveal too much . . . maybe everything so they can never be uttered out loud without choking to death on them . . . and she knows this because she's as smart as they come so she knows that I haven't figured out yet how to say — look Trixie — I don't want to give you this information — Maybe one day I will but not just yet because first of all this woman is too well known — Too shockingly famous . . . And second, I'm still so devastated by my husband's transgression that I can't mention her name out loud . . . nor can I even whisper it . . . and nor can I say that it's none of her business either — get it Trixie! — How dare you! — You — who when I was a kid wouldn't teach me how to shimmy — you just kept shimmying all around the room just to spite me — just for vengeance — laughing . . . laughing —

You who knew how to make rice pudding but would never give me the recipe — You who got everything you ever wanted *just by pointing!* . . . *everything!* no matter what the price! . . . no matter how staggering the trespassing! . . . no matter how much evil it took to *even dare to point!* — *evil!* — That's right — To dare put someone on this kind of spot but that would never stop you would it Trixie Smollens because nothing stops you, which is why I will never tell you who she is because you went too far . . . you didn't know when to stop . . . you don't know what the word "boundary" even means or how to even imagine another person's feelings . . . but too bad for you Trixie Smollens I was smoldering . . . because in the end I'm all you've got so too bad for you I was glowering as tears of rage began welling up, which meant that yes! — she won this round hands-down because tears, whether they spill or not, are always a win for the one who wasn't reduced to shedding them — right Trixie?

"So," she said the following Thursday as I walked in . . . "Any new developments with the grease-ball? — Did you find out who the mystery woman is?" she sneered, as if to say she thought that I was completely off my rocker.

"No, I still don't know," I lied as I bent to kiss her little bony face that was as slippery as ever from the years of Pond's Cold Cream she still was patting on two times a day, her chin and lower lip thrust forward as she was doing it . . . "So," she said, "where shall we have lunch today?" she mulled as she began getting slowly up, pulling herself forward by the carved wooden arms of her red velvet chair — then slowly heading toward the closet in the hall . . . that long loping gate of hers much slower all of a sudden — that great strident walk with her toes pointed slightly inward less vigorous, alarmingly so . . . "Shall we try someplace new for a change?" she asked as she looked at me quizzically like it was I — not she, who had just made this suggestion as she flung her red wool cape around her shoulders like a little old matador.

"Fine," I answered.

"What about that Greek?" she suggested as she flung her pocketbook over the opposite shoulder so that it was hanging directly in front of her belly button . . .

"Fine," I said again as we began walking slowly toward the door, her black suede shoes with the thick ridged soles trudging more slowly . . . as she put her hand in mine.

three

Curtis Hall, the assisted-living complex on the square where Trixie had been living for the past three years . . . besides being an apartment house with very small, very simple apartments that all looked out on the park; there was also a communal dining room, game rooms — sitting rooms, an emergency-room-type hospital, complete with two small operating suites, and up a short flight of concrete stairs, down a little narrow hall, and in through a thick gray door — the hospice wing where Trixie, in a sunny room immediately off the solarium, was propped up in bed, while her old maid Rosa, almost as old as she . . . sat silently in the corner reading a magazine . . .

. . . why do I come so early — why do I stay so late . . . that's the question, because for the most part now she was sleeping almost all the time . . . so what was the lure — what was I seeking that made me keep coming . . . and staying . . . almost around the clock since the day she arrived . . . as I sat down beside her bed and started waiting . . . only what was I waiting for . . . was it her wacky wisdom — her pale detached intelligence . . . or was it the last ray of hope that she'd finally reach over, put her hand on mine, and smile . . . that last little flicker of a wish that this time she'd come through for me and be the mother she never was . . . the mother I never had . . .

"This place is a madhouse," she glared as she woke with a jolt to see me sitting there. "Why have you put me here?" she leered — her same old self again — sharp as a hungry rat . . .

"Because this is where you'll have the best care and where you'll be helped to be the most comfortable," I answered.

"No, that's not the reason — You've put me here because I believe in *God*!" she snapped — "That's why!"

"No," I said as I looked at her . . . suddenly so old — so frail — so little now and shrunken . . . white as a little fishbone . . . like that tiny white translucent stick buried deep inside a piece of salmon and yet still so hideously beautiful in how willful and self-possessed every inch of her still was . . . One week ago I watched Dr. Herzog passing her death sentence — Only a week ago . . . We were sitting in his office, she in her big fur coat and big fur hat waiting silently as she looked at him — "You have an advanced lymphoma, Bea. It's everywhere," he said. "So now what we have to do is get you to the hospice center at Curtis Hall where they can care for you properly . . . It's called 'the Meadows,'" he said, "which is where my mother went when things began to get tough."

"So what!" she snapped — "What do I care where your mother went — I'm not your mother and I'm not leaving my apartment. It took me a lifetime to get there, Milton" she glared at him. "For me it's a dream-come-true to finally be smack on the square — not three blocks over, which is the story of my life — but smack right there — smack right on the square, and I have no intention of leaving," she kept glaring.

"I'm afraid you're going to have to," Dr. Herzog continued calmly with his one brown eyebrow and his one white eyebrow and his gentle patience that bespoke his enormous experience with death — "Now," he said, "we have to make sure you have the best care possible — No pain. No suffering . . . At 'the Meadows,'" he said, "you can eat anything you want at any hour, day or night — Ice cream, pizzas — even tacos around the clock — Twenty-four-hour taco service even on the weekend," he laughed as he looked at me, glad to digress for the slim second he could take from his terrible task . . . "Staffed by angels," he said, still addressing me, "the quality of the care, the kindness — all of it, the whole package is unsurpassed," he said as he grinned at Trixie. "And furthermore," he said, "there's a place for Ramona if she wants to stay overnight, and if Rosa doesn't come one day, you'll still have the best attention — everything and anything around the clock . . . The Meadows is in a class by itself," he said quietly, "which is why I'm sending you there."

"I'm not going," she said as she looked at me.

"I'm afraid you are," Dr . Herzog persisted calmly.

"I'm not going — *And That's That!*" she countered with her usual arrogant uppity self-righteousness as we sat there listening . . . And as Dr. Herzog was ringing the death knell — as he was laying it out squarely and without disguise, I was suddenly seized by a surge of almost uncontrollable rage at her. As I was listening to Dr. Herzog spelling it all out meticulously, the whole terrible story . . . I was suddenly overcome by pure raging hatred for this woman! — *my mother!* — who never once in her whole life ever lifted a finger to help me . . . *ever! — not even once!* — This woman! — *my mother!* — who never once saw or heard or cared about anything in her whole entire life except *Herself!* — This woman! — *my mother!* — who stood by and watched through half-closed eyes the slaughter of her daughter's soul and did *nothing! — Nothing!* and I hated her for this as I realized as I was sitting there that this was all I could ever hope to have — A real and powerful hatred that I was suddenly able to feel . . . Suddenly able to taste in all its terrible and overwhelming bitterness — This hatred . . . that I was suddenly able to hold in my hands like a great flaming coal and not be terrified of holding it . . . And in the great surge of vitality that holding it produced I felt a wild new freedom . . . "Wherever Dr. Herzog tells you to go is where you're going," I instructed her, coldly — blind to whatever pain — to whatever terror she might be suffering — unwilling even to register it — unimpressed, because since I was all she had, life was giving me this round . . . finally . . . Finally I was winning and she knew it as I glared at her . . . "Otherwise," I said, "things are going to get worse — Much worse," I said as I continued looking dead at her, knowing that things were already *"worse — much worse"* . . . knowing there was nothing more that anyone could do except help her to get through . . . she was beyond any other kind of help — way beyond it, and I knew it and Dr. Herzog knew it as I watched her stiffening in her chair . . . "all right," she said — not to him, but to me like a child — that profoundly courageous and hideous "all right" that accepts the unacceptable — the unbearable — "the diagnosis," which is the invisible line that separates life from death as the little crumpled wren crossed over.

Feeble, thin, emaciated . . . her white long hair hanging like thin soft feathers under her hat as I pushed her in a wheelchair the next day through the silent underbelly of Curtis Hall — that long tangle of gray basement tunnels all the way to the other side . . . and as she looked around at me as I was pushing, sunk down deep in terror in the wheelchair . . . a tiny horrified speck under her hat with her mouth half open, her neck craning so she could look around at me — this worrier . . . my mother . . . who used to ride to battle at the Rittenhouse Restaurant every Thursday on a great white charger flashing her mighty saber at me Thursday-in and Thursday-out . . . rain or shine . . . the battle she loved so much — the warring — the ferocious display of rage and contempt — the teasing, the insults, and always flaunting her victories like how she knew how to make rice pudding and wouldn't teach me . . . or how to shimmy ha! ha! ha! . . . all of it history now — all of it gone except the terror she had of death and the rage I had at her — my mother — who might have wanted to love me but she couldn't . . . me . . . her only child . . . this daughter she was stuck with . . . it wasn't in her nature, or as she put it, "she was too old when I was born," — or — "she did the best she could," both she told me so often that together they became a kind of mantle of glory she wore like a tiara of good intent that excused and absolved her of every meanness — every blindness — every withholding.

"Some people say you shouldn't say everything that's on your mind, but I say say what you want and what I have to say is that I regret *Nothing*!" she glared at me, still reeking of *that venerated air of supreme indifference* that she so diligently cultivated over her whole long nasty life as she looked at me now from this next leg of her journey, her bed in 'the Meadows' at Curtis Hall, where broad beams of white sunlight filled with dancing flecks of dust flooded the whole brilliantly sunny room . . .

"Is everything all right — Are you able to sleep?" I asked; the usual kind of question when you can't ask what you really want to know — when you can't get near all that hidden business that lies waiting in there that no one's ever able to ask because no one knows when or how or where to even begin . . . *"Of course I'm able to sleep,"* she snapped as she looked at me like I was insane — "In order to sleep all you have to do is start snoring, and if that doesn't work," she said, "then you have to pretend you're an egg in a nest and a big fat hen is sitting on you," she remarked offhandedly from deep inside her pillows looking gruesomely transformed — her hands crossed over the lacy top of her pink nightgown like two dry old leaves that were about to dissolve . . . leaves that someone had once pressed in a book in order to keep and preserve them that now had become mummified —

She had become so thin because eating had become too much of an ordeal, even the sight of food had begun to revolt her . . . nothing, not even chocolate or Turkish halvah, which she once loved, could dent the wall that had formed around her appetite — She said she couldn't taste; it was gone she said so I'd hold the piece of chocolate or the chunk of halvah up to her nose and tell her to take a deep sniff, which she would do obediently, like a child . . . then she'd shake her head like "what's the use" as I'd watch carefully . . . too carefully . . . almost as though I was trying to watch time . . . not her . . . but rather, watching hours and minutes and seconds as though I was watching against death . . . looking . . . watching . . . fascinated by watching her dying . . . and yet terrified to be gazing directly into the dragon's mouth myself, because as I was watching her I was watching my own death too and the death of the whole world and everything in it — every tree — every plant, every flower — every cat and dog and bird and bug that ever lived and breathed and stretched its limbs in the warmth of the sun that ever was and ever will be that was dying with her like the whole world was dying with her the same as I was dying with her because she was my mother . . . the one who gave me life the same as she gave me death whether I liked it or not — whether I liked life or not — whether I liked her or hated her or loved her with all my heart it didn't matter anymore because she was in me and that's what I was losing — that part of myself that was going with her that would never come back — not ever because that's the price you pay — the price you have to pay . . . as my preoccupation with her began consuming me as her illness began speeding up . . . It was all suddenly happening so fast . . . It was all suddenly racing so ruthlessly . . . as more and more she became all I could think about . . . all I could feel was sadness . . . all there was was sadness — a terrible huge heartbreaking sadness . . . a scary dire terrible sadness because she gave me death the same as she gave me life until finally that's who she finally was . . . everything and everyone . . . every plant and every flower and every bug and bird that ever lived and breathed and withered in the glare of death . . . as her pale detachment and her great old age were honing her finally into something close to perfect and yet she was still alive, and since perfection belongs to only death . . . now I was terrified that I'd never find the mother I never had . . . that she was lost somewhere in the tide that was going out as I suddenly wanted to hear every word she ever uttered — know every thought she ever thought before all her words got garbled — before all her thoughts got fuzzy and started running all together in a mix of dreams and waking that was all going too fast away from me . . . everything racing too fast away because I wasn't ready — no! as I tried to hold on to what I hated and cursed so much, so long, so unrelentingly — this mean little harsh survivor who would never stop fighting — who would never concede the throne — who would struggle on with every drop of strength she had to live and go on living — half blind, nearly deaf, cancer-riddled, and so withered and emaciated that it was hard to have to look at the knees of her matchstick legs that instantly buckled if she tried to stand on them and yet she kept fighting, fighting — battered, torn, failing, and yet struggling on heroically with unbeliev-able will . . . still the ferocious worrier, courageous and brave, which is what made it all the more terrible to have to see because as ragged and ravaged as she was, the last thing in the world she wanted was to die, which is why I started coming every day, day in and day out . . . to bear witness . . . to honor her and to honor the war she was waging, this final war, the real war now that she was battling with so much astonishing courage and even more astonishing dignity . . . but was that really why I kept coming day after day . . . was that really what I wanted to watch . . . or was it that I wanted to watch her finally lose . . . watch something finally get her — did I want to watch her fighting the unvanquished with my own two eyes . . . I had to be suspicious, I had to ask myself this question — was that the real secret of why I kept coming day after day — day in and day out . . . or even worse, was it yet again the "dutiful daughter" myth . . . the lie . . . yet again another lie . . . that hid the ordinary everyday nothingness between us . . . Two strangers, my mother and I, who in the end more or less tolerated each other, but only barely, we didn't choose each other — we "got" each other and the result was, after all was said and done — *nothing* — something like seeing for the first time the inside of a tire that blew on the way to Maine one year . . . and the shock . . . how stunned I was to see that there was *nothing* inside the thick black rubber frame — *nothing at all . . . nothing! . . .* my mother and I were an accident of fate, mismatched and not remotely understanding of the other except for the fact that we both were living creatures, and as such were heir to what all living creatures are heir to . . . other than that, the two of us were always and forever strangers, stuck with each other for the journey, like the person you're sitting next to on a plane.

four

I stayed all night as she grew worse . . . became more confused, disoriented — didn't know what time it was, or even if it was night or day . . . Finally she became too weak to sit up in bed — thought Mr. Columbus was her long-dead brother Albert whom she told to go in the other room and take a nap, her teeth were out now all the time — her hearing aid permanently in a dish on the table next to her as she looked at me . . . helplessly, like a terrified child . . . staring at me with a wild glint in her eye . . . as though she could see the horror of her coming dissolution . . . her defeat coming inch by inch . . . minute by minute to drag her by her entrails into eternity.

Only a few weeks before while she still had, as she said, "the strength of a prizefighter," and was looking for a little fracas — a little rumble — nothing much, just enough to keep her perking . . . on that last Thursday when I came for lunch (we weren't going out anymore, now Rosa was bringing a tray into her bedroom) . . . as I sat in the little flowered chair across from her while she was propped up in bed, I began asking questions because now was the time to find out everything I could . . . Now, while she still seemed invulnerable — fierce — undaunted I began questioning her . . . carefully, very carefully — careful not to incur her wrath . . . careful not to arouse her suspicions — careful not to

enrage her by making her suspect that I might want
something — anything . . . "Ah ha," she'd smolder . . .
"out to fleece me on my deathbed, is she? — Well, we'll
see about that!" would be her response to the merest
suggestion of my wanting even a bit of information . . .
and not just from me, but me in particular, because I was
the one she suspected of every treachery — everything
sinister . . . even more sinister — even more deadly and
dangerous than even Rosa . . . as I cleared my throat,
"so tell me Trixie," I said offhandedly, "what's the secret
of your fantastic magnetism and all that alluring appeal
you have that time has done nothing to alter?" I asked,
thinking how everyone wants to be a self-centered
egomaniac like Trixie, but how many really ever can?

"Indifference," she snapped swift and calmly . . .
"Cold, bloodless *Indifference* — What those Orientals
call *Detachment*! — The *'I don't care!'* philosophy," she
smoldered as she stared blankly off into space, enraged
at being asked a question — any question . . . but since
I was being cagey . . . so far there wasn't a hair of suspicion that I might want more . . . including even maybe
some advice, god forbid so I kept going . . . slowly . . .
very slowly . . . trying to eke out whatever little crumbs
I could . . .

"But what if you *Do* care?" I asked gingerly.

"Then you must pretend you *Don't* — It's called *The
Great 'As If'* technique," she snapped . . . "Number one
— you must act *'As If'* you don't care about *Anything*!"
she glared at me, her face toward me now and thrust

slightly forward with a surprising look of intense concentration as though she were being interviewed on *Meet the Press* . . . "That's number one . . . Number two," she said, snared now on her own petard of egoism . . . irresistibly caught on a form of boasting she couldn't resist — "always remain *Distant!*" she said contemptuously — "always be *Haughty* — and always — *Always! no matter what* — *Withhold* . . . *Because Withholding Is Power* — *Remember that!* which means you give nothing to anyone under any circumstances, including *Information*," she kept glaring — "Does that answer your question — Now may I eat my lunch?" This old lady with her long white hair, thin and straggly now . . . her thin blue arms like tissue paper with everything showing through — veins, blood vessels — nothing hidden anymore — it was too late for all of that with her little bony withers wrapped in a red cashmere shawl sunk deep into her pillows living now under the constant eye of her maid Rosa who tiptoed over with her cup of tea — silently putting it on the tray in front of her and then quietly tiptoeing away —

"As I Suspected!" she seethed as she looked at the tea . . . "I could have told you *At a Glance* that this tea would be *Ice Cold* — *Again!*" she began ranting as she looked at it — "How many times do I have to tell you — *Dummy!* that you have to let the water come to a *Full Fast Boil First* — *Before* you put the tea bag in — Is that too hard for you to understand?" she was seething at Rosa — all the veins in her neck sticking out . . . as Rosa, her dark

round maid, fat and kind like a jolly bowling ball, was half bending — half standing over her, as she began smiling joyously as she was being yelled at, which Rosa cheerfully considered part of what she was being paid for — to be insulted, taunted, and badgered maliciously, which enraged and embarrassed me — I didn't know where to look . . . but not Rosa . . . oh no, she just kept smiling as if she were thinking . . . "this here Miss Bea Smollens is some fabulous somebody all right — '*a queen!*'" she seemed to be glowing with a secret inner joy that came from being so brainwashed by Trixie that by now she didn't know who this woman even was — maybe a queen — maybe a goddess — maybe a rare work of art — a treasure . . . as I watched fascinated by how she did it every time . . . what was her trick . . . how did she get away with it . . . yelling at decent people . . . giving nothing — doing nothing — never lifting a finger — bullying people — pushing them around like they were dirt . . . and all the time the *rage!* — always the hideous *rage* . . . which was all she really had to give . . . *rage!* and yet everyone who came near her became an adoring slave . . .

"There's something you're not telling me," I smiled, "some little secret something that's the key to all that extraordinary power you have locked in there . . . what is it Trixie?" I smiled again.

"*Acceptance!*" she snapped impatiently — "It's the Secret to Everything!" she sneered as she stared arrogantly off into space — "Which means you have to accept things the way they *Are — Not the Way You Want*

Them To Be — Which means you have to play the hand you're *Dealt* — *Get it?*" she glared as a new boiling-hot cup of tea was placed on the tray in front of her that she scrutinized meticulously and then, seeing the steam, she commanded Rosa to begin scratching her foot as she took a sip . . .

"But what about a little peace and calm? How can you have any peace and calm — any sense of well-being if things aren't right in your life — ?"

"First of all . . . Things are *never* 'right in your life,' so don't even bother — That's the first thing . . . And as for *'peace and calm'* — They're the two worst things *on Earth*! — They mean *Nothing*! — You might as well be *dead* if that's what you're looking for," she snapped angrily as she stared off into space . . . clearly I was annoying her, my questions were annoying her . . . the whole conversation was annoying her so I had to step it up . . . "Okay — one more question, a quickie," I said nervously — as I was warming up for the big one . . .

"Well — What is it? — go on," she said irritated as she slowly began sipping her tea.

"What if Mr. Columbus has someone?" I said — "I don't have to accept *that,* do I?"

"Oh for god's *Sake!*" she blasted me again — "Back to that repulsive oily *Jerk*! — *Your revolting husband — Again!*" her jealousy toward him like it was toward anyone I cared about, soaring wildly out of control because for as far back as I could remember she couldn't take it if I loved anyone but her . . .

"Back to that grease-ball *Jerk* who you still believe has someone — Well, tell me Ramona — who in her right mind would even *look* at him? — But okay, what if he does? — Let's just say for argument's sake he does . . . *Then Yes! Of course you must accept it because you must accept Everything . . . Without Exception — Period!*" she glared at me as she motioned Rosa to scratch harder — dig her nails *harder* into her foot as she made a clawlike gesture with one hand implying a little *fierceness please!* as Rosa's scratching was becoming a little limp and distracted because she was hanging on to every word of our conversation with her eyes and mouth wide open . . . The idea of having any privacy with Trixie — the notion of confidentiality — of intimacy, a joke . . . this woman was like a house that had no doors or windows — everything blowing everywhere without constraints — unchecked — uncensored . . . "There's nothing you can do," she went on, her foot now being scratched to her satisfaction as she took a sip of tea . . . "you have no choice . . . So yes, you *must accept it*! — And then you must make yourself *Not Care! — Period!*" she said, "which is the whole entire point of being *Alive! — Not to give a hoot!*"

"But what about my marriage?"

"Yes? So — What about it?" she said as she as she took another sip.

"How can I accept that my husband has a mistress who is so much more beautiful — so much more brilliant, so much sexier than I could ever even dream of being . . . Someone who has *everything*!"

"Oh for god's *Sake!*" she snapped as she looked away, only this time she said it with such complete disgust — such total abhorrent contempt and revulsion that I was immediately sorry . . . sorry I turned to her . . . sorry I asked for *something! — anything!* from this woman who couldn't give anything . . . it wasn't in her . . . it wasn't her style . . . she was too stingy — too withholding . . . too *fundamentally spiteful to give anybody anything except her rage!* . . . Did I forget this — Did I forget who I was dealing with — Didn't I know the story . . . So why did I keep trying — What was wrong with me . . . Come on Ramona, I admonished myself as I got up to leave as she suddenly put up her hand to stop me . . . "Go out and get a cloth doll and seven hat pins with black tops at any five-and-ten," she muttered . . . "Try! to find out this vixen's name — at least her first name — Then name the doll for her with some little naming ceremony . . . you know, candles, incense — a few little chants here and there that you can make up as you go along, but *make sure* this chanting includes the vixen's name *seven times!* — Then," she said — "turn out all the lights — pull down all the shades — close the curtains — make sure it's very dark in there — *pitch black* . . . except of course for the seven candles — *don't touch them!*" she said as she suddenly sat bolt upright in her bed as if some strange something had suddenly taken hold of her . . . her long white hair, wild and thin like a fuzzy incandescent mist glowing all around her head as she stared at me not blinking — "you must leave them all burning Ramona!"

she muttered — "Do you understand?" she asked . . . transfixed . . . as she continued staring at me . . . her eyes not blinking now . . . "— you must use seven candles — not six — not eight . . . only seven because seven is the magic number of new beginnings, which will give you a little extra power as you begin sticking in the pins . . . I've always found that right between the eyes or directly into the crotch are the most effective spots," she said as she continued glaring at me . . . "Either location will take away the spell this vixen has cast over that oily putz — *Ich!*" she said still glaring blindly at me without blinking . . . "But never mind — if you're seeking my advice . . . then you must do *exactly* what I say down to the letter," she said, "and that greasy putz — *Ich!* very shortly will wonder what he ever saw in whoever she is before an outright revulsion for her suddenly takes over . . . and this change will occur *exactly* seven hours after the first pinprick . . . remember the number seven," she said as she continued staring at me without blinking as though she was staring blindly into space . . . "Remember," she whispered, "that the most secret secret of all secrets is the magic number *Seven!*" she kept whispering — "or anything that has a seven in it — like seventeen or twenty-seven or seventy-five — *get it?*" she mumbled . . . as she suddenly sank back into her pillows, exhausted, closed her eyes — put the back of her hand over her forehead, sighed . . . and then with her eyes still closed she began smiling broadly and nodding as if to someone who might have also known this dark secret remedy — this black art — *Her colossus!* as she began muttering "yes," as she continued nodding and smiling to god knows who . . . "Indeed Yes!" she smiled with her eyes still closed — "Indeed I'm here to help because I'm her mother am I not?" she was smiling with her eyes still closed. "And yes," she said, "that greasy jerk — *Sephardic Jews* — *Ich!* is unfortunately her husband, which means in plain English that *yes she must* protect him — *Ich!* with those disgusting fingers — *Ich!* how can she stand to have those fingers touch her — *Ich!*" she said as she opened her eyes and turned toward me — suddenly back to her old self — *completely back!* — "You know what they remind me of," she snapped — "But I'm a decent woman. I do what's right when called upon," she said, impressed with her extremely magnanimous behavior in having decided to yes, bestow on me her secret voodoo magic, which I knew she had been dabbling in for years because I used to find hat pins with black tops and half-burned candles all over the house — but she came through — in the end, when the chips were down . . . in her own strange way she tried to help me and my troubled marriage to a man she loathed and detested . . . and why did she detest him so? — because I loved him . . . which meant that if I loved someone — *anyone!* — there might not be enough for her . . .

"So okay!" she went on — "I'll take your word for it that someone *might be* after that dark oily putz — *Ich!* which means that yes — of course you must step in because that's what marriage is . . . Protecting each other," she said as she glared at me — "and believe-you-me," she scoffed as she looked over at Rosa who was dozing in the other chair, "I know what I'm talking about, because believe-you-me," she scoffed again as her eyes moved over to the window, "I had to stick plenty of pins into plenty of dolls to protect your father from plenty of things . . . various sex-crazed women — the flu, blinking yellow lights, impetigo, blizzards — infections, hailstones the size of golf balls, psoriasis — goniffs of every kind — those despicable friends of his he used to play poker with every Sunday afternoon . . . and why? — because your father *protected Me*," she glared as though her look was a challenge because they were lies! . . . all lies . . . she was lying through her teeth again . . . again . . . as I remembered her blue satin stocking box in the top drawer of her dresser where she used to stash the few little dollars she could pinch that he once pulled her hair and almost broke her arm trying to retrieve . . .

"And who protected me?" I asked as I remembered every night . . . night after night after night . . . Nathan Smollens . . . walking stiffly into my bedroom like a zombie whose legs don't bend as it just keeps coming . . . coming . . . oblivious to where he was . . . oblivious to what he was doing . . . unstoppable — fierce and hideous like he was in some kind of awful trance . . . every night . . . night after night after night . . . as he'd grab me as I started kicking and scratching as I began screaming for her . . . screaming . . . screaming . . . every night . . . every single night . . .

"You?" she laughed as she looked at me . . . "Protect you from *What*? — Protect you from *Whom*? — You didn't need protection . . . *We adored you*," she said . . .

"And your father," she said as she rolled her eyes . . . "Maybe too much if you ask me!"

five

The call from Dr. Herzog came at ten at night — He said we had to come right away — she had no pressure he said and blood was pouring out of her backside faster than they were able to keep putting it in . . .

. . . and in the blue stillness of the emergency room where there were no windows . . . no sounds . . . no time . . . behind a thin blue curtain she was smiling peacefully, her long white hair in a wide blue plastic shower cap as I came over from the nurses' station where I had begun to make whatever arrangements that were necessary . . . "where are you going at this hour?" she asked even though she had no clue what the hour was or if it was even night or day.

"I'm on my way to New York," I said — "Just thought I'd drop in to say good-bye before I left . . ."

"Good-bye," she said, busy with her long-dead brother Albert . . . her long-dead mother . . . her mother's sister Rose — Rose's daughter little Pauline who died when she was two . . . all of them sitting at the foot of her bed whom she said she was too busy visiting with to talk to me right now . . . "Come back when I have more time," she said as she raised her thin blue hand to wave good-bye . . . this person I've sat next to on the plane for so long a journey . . . my mother . . . watching when I was little from the window in the living room as she was making her way down the icy steps out front . . . watching her clinging to the black iron rail . . . watching her terror of slipping . . . and understanding for the first time then, as I was watching her, with tears streaming down my face . . . that there's such a thing as death.

part seven

caught

one

At the top of a great flight of winding white marble stairs, an enormous bedroom — huge and beckoning in ice-blue satin like a gigantic perfect diamond that whispers of money, wealth, and power . . . with mirrored walls and little mirrored tables and ice-blue satin chairs . . . and heavy ice-blue satin drapes trimmed all down the front with thick blue satin balls drooping across the rug like fairy ornaments . . . The whole room rigid and unyielding, like the chilling beauty of certain odorless orchids that bloom only in the night . . .

And in the middle of it all — the Bed . . . huge and terrifying in all its scary implications . . . looming like a challenge — like a threat . . . softened by the presence of countless thick fur coats . . . a whole mountain of minks and sables . . . those almost living things . . . alive but not quite and yet still lending something in the way of comfort and companionship to this steely silent ice-blue world where everything was still . . . unshattered . . . as though time somehow stopped just at the door and began whispering in a completely different voice . . . hushed and muffled . . . about sex . . . and accomodations made and ambitions realized that you could almost hear if you listened carefully . . . this fortress bedroom . . . this bastion of the enduring deal as I slipped in, took off my shoes, got on their huge blue satin bed . . . pulled a bunch of thick mink coats over me until I was completely buried . . . and then . . .

as I lay back, with the perfume on the furs wafting up like sweet drifts of roses and lilies on a summer night I closed my eyes . . . while downstairs . . . blaring on and on like it did every year . . . year after year . . . Harry Stain's gala New Year's Eve extravaganza — where to be or not to be invited was the measure in Philadelphia of who you were . . . and who were we? — Mr. and Mrs. Chicken-and-Eggs of the Entire Universe!

two

Harry Stain looked like a great bird of prey . . . a hawk maybe or an eagle with thick tinted glasses that gave his doughy face a kind of permanently unfocused glare . . . A world-famous collector of contemporary art, every New Year's Eve he and his wife Lulubelle gave a party to celebrate their latest acquisitions as Harry Stain wandered aimlessly among his guests — smiling . . . Long ago he was a theatrical lawyer — made a killing in the market, retired from law and began collecting art, a natural result he said, of his lifelong passion for color; as a child he was often seen running around naked he'd say, with a bunch of Crayola crayons stuck in his behind — a sure sign he'd say — of the budding art collector he was destined to become.

As for Lulubelle, an identical twin and formerly a raving beauty with thick red hair and a fast easy laugh . . . but now, from living so long with this coldly brilliant, slow-moving little tank whose main duty as host was to stick his tongue down as many women's throats as he could while he simultaneously felt their butts, she finally turned to stone as though the fierce emotional aloneness she endured . . . his colossal philandering — or both . . . was the price she paid . . . something like having a terrible illness that left her never fully recovered, but rather, merely hanging on to a life that gave her little besides the money . . . and this decision, apparently to opt for the gold froze her into something with fastened lips that never seemed to move anymore — not even when she was talking — not even when she laughed — her red flaming hair now a short white bob — her fast easy laugh, a scowl . . . until finally, the once gorgeous Lulubelle O'Donnell-Stain was all dried up — stiff, wrinkled, and sour as though she'd turned into a foreboding shore against the wild tide of her sinister husband's immense flamboyancy.

Their enormous home, a huge rambling white stucco mansion the size of an elementary school, was at the end of a four-minute drive that went snaking all the way up a long winding hill where two huge black iron gates at the top would slowly creak open as you pushed a button and spoke into a little metal box . . . and then . . . entering into their world in the middle of the night was like entering into the dark underbelly of the First Pennsylvania Bank and Trust, where everybody who passed through those formidable gates was instantly transformed into infinitesimal bugs with little blue pathetic legs creeping bravely forward to peer up the skirt of the monster lady who sat up there showing everything . . . the monster lady who kept laughing uproariously as everyone kept trying to get a better look . . . a better peek . . . into all her secret crevices — her thick wood-beamed ceilings — her great gaping fireplaces — her furniture and art and sculpture and all her fancy ashtrays as the little bugs all drank champagne passed on silver trays, their antennae darting wildly as they nibbled caviar from huge silver urns as they kept rubbing their hind legs together to make all those little fake-laughing sounds — all those fake-gay and marvelous fake noises of gratitude as their antennae kept darting . . . darting . . . looking everywhere to see who they were rubbing up against . . . who was who, as they kept eating and looking and fake-laughing until I could sneak away, go upstairs — sneak into that silent ice-blue bedroom that was something like the top of the world — the Arctic Circle . . . or maybe the top of the Himalayas, same as I had done last year and the year before that and the year before that . . . kick off my shoes, sink into that soft blue satin bed, pull a bunch of mink coats over me until I was completely buried . . . and then . . . just lie there listening to the far-off sound of voices like a low hum that comes and goes like waves, dotted every now and then by the sound of a door banging somewhere . . . the far-off sound of a car driving away across the gravel . . . as the dimness of the room began sprouting things . . . little objects beginning to emerge like minor characters in a play . . . a painting of a pale blue lady in a thick gold frame . . . cut-crystal perfume bottles on a mirrored dressing table next to a pair of silver scissors with blue jeweled handles . . . a crystal box on the mirrored dressing table filled with little crystal balls . . . mirrored night tables on either side of the bed with long thin reading lamps like giant robots rising awkwardly out of a sea of silent people peering out of countless little silver frames . . . a picture of Harry Stain in his thick tinted glasses grinning in a tuxedo — a young bald Harry Stain in his thick tinted glasses in tennis clothes smiling by the net, his hand on his hip with the gorgeous redheaded Lulubelle in tennis clothes beside him — Harry Stain in his thick tinted glasses smiling with the mayor — a more formal Harry Stain in his thick tinted glasses in a business suit sitting with one arm resting on his desk . . . laughing Harry Stain sitting with the once wildly beautiful Lulubelle and Harry Belafonte — Harry Stain in his thick tinted glasses laughing with Lucille Ball and Desi Arnaz . . . a gorgeous Lulubelle and her gorgeous identical twin sister Annabelle smiling in long black evening gowns, each with her single strand of long white pearls . . . a formal portrait of the whole Stain family — all their smiling children and all their smiling dogs, all with the same dark curly hair . . . how come they all looked so happy . . . joyful — how did they do it — what was their trick I wondered as I gazed at all those framed testimonials of so much success . . . all those happy laughing photographs — how does it happen — all that happiness . . . wondering if Lulubelle Stain when she was young, when she was my age thirty years ago . . . was she wild in bed . . . or was she like me — a liar from the very start because she had a secret too — a heartbreaking tragedy too . . . that didn't allow her to feel a thing — not ever . . . so she faked it too — just like me . . . from the very start . . .

. . . wondering if ever once in her whole life she ever

wanted one wild night with a garage mechanic caught in the grip of a desire so intense that she was powerless to fight it . . . wondering if she ever tore out of her house in the middle of the night searching for someone — *anyone!* broken and disheveled because the hunger in her was so powerful that it made her sick, only to come home empty-handed so to speak . . . wondering if she ever craved and craved and craved until the craving drove her crazy . . . if she ever in her whole existence had the urge to risk it all for a single transgression that might have cost her everything . . . wondering if she ever felt things like that . . . or did she love money too much — or her children too much . . . or her home too much . . . or her life or her pearls or her gigantic paintings and all her big thick hunks of pitch-black sculpture — or just being safe . . . was that what she clung to the same as I . . . to just being safe — or maybe it just wasn't in her — that thing . . . or maybe Harry Stain could make it happen for her . . . or maybe she never had desires like that in the first place . . . wondering if there are such women . . . gorgeous women like Lulubelle Stain who don't need a man because they diddle themselves . . . or diddle with their girlfriends in the afternoon while they drink a little gin . . . or maybe they didn't need to diddle because maybe long ago someone killed it in her too . . . maybe someone scared her so badly when she was young that something in her froze . . . so many articles that say that at least forty percent of all women never feel a thing — nothing . . . and they're too

ashamed to tell because of the shame . . . the shame . . .
the humiliation as I close my eyes — the "disgrace"
of being "frigid" . . . so they just keep it to themselves
that they couldn't measure up . . . because like me they
don't know how to tell . . . they don't know who to
tell . . . who can you talk to about such things . . . how
can you dare . . . until finally you just keep faking it or
else pretending someday it'll change or else pretending
that it doesn't matter anyhow . . . like I pretend . . . or
maybe Harry Stain killed it in her — that wildness . . .
wondering how many women really have it anyhow . . .
and if they do . . . how many hold on to it . . . not
counting what you see in the movies . . . all those lying
deceiving glamour liars — all lies anyhow . . . lies — lies
— all their lies that we grew up on . . . all their lies that
ruined all of us — what a joke . . . as my eyes are getting
heavy . . . bleary . . . sleepy . . . sleepy . . . sleep as the
mirrored bathroom door suddenly flies open. . .

. . . the smell of gardenia perfume suddenly filling the
room — shattering the stillness like breaking glass . . .

. . . as I peer out from under all the coats . . .

. . . to see those white satin shoes all right . . .

. . . that long white chiffon evening gown with the one
thick rhinestone strap all right . . . walking slowly out
of the bathroom . . .

. . . as she's lifting her long red wavy hair to the top of her head . . . and holding it there a moment . . . and then letting it fall . . .

. . . watching — barely able to breathe from the shock . . . as she goes over to the mirrored dressing table . . . pulls out the little blue satin chair and sits down . . .

. . . watching . . . as she takes a little silver comb out of her evening bag and starts combing that gorgeous long red wavy hair . . .

. . . watching . . . as she takes out a small canister of Invisible-Net Hair Spray and gives a little squirt . . . watching . . . as she puts the hair spray and the comb back in her bag . . .

. . . watching . . . as she takes out her long gold lipstick — takes off the top, twists it up . . . and then carefully covers her thick red gorgeous lips — smears them together and then stares at herself in the mirror — lost in the depths of concentration . . .

. . . watching . . . as she closes the lipstick and then cocks her head to one side and gazes at herself as she smiles . . .

. . . watching . . . as she fluffs her wavy hair as she stands up slowly, turns, and starts walking toward me . . . *not*

suspecting! — never! — not in her wildest imagination . . .
that I . . . her lover's wife! . . . Mrs. Solomon Columbus is
lurking under all the coats . . .

. . . as she keeps coming slowly toward me . . .

. . . watching . . . as she stops beside the bed that's in
front of one of the mirrored walls . . . and begins carefully examining herself again . . . head-to-foot . . .

. . . watching . . . as she smooths her white chiffon gown
carefully across her hips as she's smiling . . .

. . . watching . . . as she fluffs her hair . . . again . . .

. . . watching as she opens her evening bag . . . takes out
a little bottle of perfume, puts the bag on the bed so
close to me that I can touch it . . .

. . . watching . . . as she puts a few little drops behind
each ear . . . watching as she puts the bottle back into
her bag . . . as the whole room reeks even more of that
same gardenia perfume that's always on Mr. Columbus's
shirts . . . always in his hair and on his hands that permeates our whole apartment every night . . . as she's turning her head slightly to the right . . . then putting both
hands on her hips again . . . and smiling . . .

. . . watching as she licks her lips . . . watching as she cocks her head slightly back and over to the side as she keeps smiling at herself — her long red wavy hair tumbling perfectly past her shoulders . . . pleased with her hair . . . pleased with her white satin evening shoes . . . pleased . . . with her strapless white chiffon gown with the one rhinestone strap going over the other shoulder . . . as she keeps staring at herself trying to decide which is more beautiful . . . her body . . . or her face . . . as I see the silver scissors with the blue jeweled handles gleaming on Lulubelle Stain's dressing table . . . beckoning . . .

. . . and while she's staring at herself in the mirror and smiling . . . I slither on my back down under all the coats down to the bottom of the bed like a commando, then silently I drop to the floor . . . crawl softly as low as I can across the pale blue carpet over to the dressing table before Mr. Columbus gets up here *because of course he'll be here any second . . . of course . . . to be with her . . . of course . . . to knock a fast one off while no one's looking* . . . as I reach up and snatch the scissors, slither back on my belly so she doesn't see my reflection in any of the mirrored walls . . . this prism room of mirrors upon mirrors like the inside of a gigantic kaleidoscope of reflection upon reflection upon reflection . . . and as she's still smiling at herself . . . as she's licking her lips again and smoothing her dress I jump up — quick! — hurry! . . . no time to waste! . . . the scissors pointing at her back . . . "sorry Rita," I whisper as I leap forward and raise my hand with the scissors clutched in it . . .

———

"Where were you? — Where have you *been*?" he asks as he suddenly appears in the door . . . "What's going on?" he says as he looks at me —

"Will you tell me *Please!* — *What in God's name are you doing?*" he asks as she slips out so fast, so seamlessly . . . that it's almost as though she were a phantom in a dream.

three

"Tell me the truth! — *Please!* — *I have to know!* — Am I crazy or do you have someone — Someone who wears heavy gardenia perfume . . . Someone you went upstairs to meet — Someone you can't live without *fucking Mr. Columbus!* — Admit that either a crime has been committed against our family . . . *or I'm completely out of my Mind!* — *Please!* — *Tell me the Truth* — *Because knowing and yet not knowing is driving me Insane . . ."*

. . . but he won't answer . . . he won't tell me . . . he won't say a word . . . not one sound as he's driving in a fierce and hideous silence — his whole body rigid, unyielding with those ten fat red penis fingers gripping the steering wheel like the talons of an eagle . . . Solomon Columbus, the quintessential Jewish man — the walking conscience of all humanity . . . which is why he's so reviled — so abhorred because he's the necessary other — the silent outsider — solemn and apart — listening to no one, adhering to nothing but his own private God of "Thou Shalt Not" as he keeps walking gravely onward through all the ages . . . alone and somber — the keeper of all the gates as he keeps driving through the freezing night with not one word . . . not one sound all the way into the city . . . all the way into our garage — his weapon — his battle cry — Silence!

". . . I saw her with my own two *Eyes!*" I'm screaming

— *"So Please!"* I'm begging him as we're hanging up our coats in the closet in the hall . . . "have the decency *to Help Me . . . !"*

. . . but he won't answer . . . he doesn't say a word . . . not as we're brushing our teeth . . . not as he's getting into his blue nightshirt . . . not as he's brushing his hair . . . nothing . . . not one word from this man who just by telling me the simple truth, I can live . . . as I look at him — and as I look at him I realize . . . that it's the lie! — the lie is what's important — The lie is all that counts! . . . in other words — not getting caught means more to him than I as he holds back the covers for me to get into bed like a gentleman holds open a door . . . as the barbed luminous agony . . . the shrill spiked pain of knowing what I know I know . . . coupled with finally realizing who he really is as I'm standing in my red flannel nightgown beside the bed still hoping that if I give him one more chance . . . only one more chance . . . that magic "one more chance" . . . *"please!"* I'm begging him again . . . "if you have the *guts*! . . . for god's sake — *save me!* — save my sanity . . ."

"For the hundred thousandth time" he shouts — *"There's No One!* — I don't have *Anyone! — Period!"*

"Then tell me . . . as if I didn't know, who that redheaded woman was who flew out of the room the second you walked in . . . a certain flamboyant redheaded *love*

Goddess who dances a wild flamenco . . . you see Mr. Columbus, I even know who she is," I whisper . . .

"You're *Nuts!*" he glares at me from deep inside the covers . . . "You're completely *Out of your mind! — Cuckoo!*" he glares . . .

"*Never Admit! which is the cardinal rule of every cheat whose whole aim in life is to get away with something —* which means that it's the lie — the lie is all that matters isn't it Mr. Columbus — the lie — like a huge gleaming diamond — bright and hopeful that matters more to you than I which means that that's who you're really married to — the lie — not me," I'm shouting as I'm glaring back, knowing as I'm shouting that she would *Never* behave this way . . . *Never!* . . . which is why she would make a better wife for him — because in all her icy perfectness she would always be controlled . . . *WOULDN'T YOU RITA?* . . . which would make you always win . . . *WOULDN'T IT* . . . So go on — marry her — why don't you? — She would never behave like this . . . She would never yell and shout if she gets upset and what's more . . . she'd always come through for you in bed with all those tricks — all those bumps and grinds and little twirls she does with her hips as she tosses her head around in wild passionate madness with *nothing fake!* — No! Not with her — Oh No!

". . . with her it's always the real McCoy isn't it Solomon Columbus — and not just once but every single time — am I right? — Isn't every single time with her *Pure Ecstasy?* — Answer me!" I shout . . .

"Stop — For God's sake!" he shouts — *"Will You Stop!"*

"No! — Not until you admit you're running around . . . I have a nose you know, that smells that heavy gardenia perfume the minute you walk in the door at night . . . that heavy gardenia perfume that's all over all your clothes and in your hair and on your hands that permeates our whole apartment the minute you come in which is the same perfume I smelled up there tonight — and furthermore . . . I know that smell Mr. Columbus — I wasn't born yesterday you know — It's the smell of a woman who'll splash that perfume on and then dance a wild flamenco . . . Then splash on some more, drive you wild with desire, dump you and then splash on some more as she goes on to the next poor sap — then the next poor chump and then the next and then the next because that's what they're like Solomon Columbus! — all those wild flamenco Hollywood love goddesses — only goddesses don't return your love because goddesses don't return *Anything*! — *They Can't!* — It isn't in them because they're too busy being goddesses — too busy being wildly desired all the time because they can't live without that kind of adoration for even *a single second* . . . so beware Solomon Columbus," I'm warning him . . . "today it's you — tomorrow the Ali Khan — the next day Orson Welles and then after that who knows . . . Victor Mature . . . Jack Palance . . . one after the other they come and one after another she chews them up — spits them out and then goes on to the next . . . which isn't love! — *It's a demand for love which is really Hate! . . ."*

"You're completely *Nuts!*" he says — "Everything in your head is scrambled eggs . . . You've lost it," he laughs from deep inside his pillow where he's all curled up — "And anyhow," he says, "it's a known fact," he laughs, "that infidelity saves more marriages than it breaks."

"Ah — Ha! . . . At last!" . . . you're about to come clean . . .

"At long last! — Bravo Solomon Columbus!" I shout joyfully . . . happy and grateful for even the smallest peek into that place where the truth is waiting bright and big and magnificent . . . grateful for even one little hint of it — grateful for even the smallest little crumb to grab on to like a life raft so I won't go under from all the deceit and tricks and lies that are swimming in my head in gigantic ever-widening wakes — gigantic all-consuming wakes that I'm afraid will drown me if he won't come clean . . .

. . . which it looks like he's going to do — It looks like he's finally putting out a hand to me . . . so thanks I smile as I began to collect myself — get a little jump on all the madness, as I squeeze out another little smile for him that still feels more like begging than real relief . . .

"Anything else on your mind?" he says as he looks me dead in the eye as he props himself up on one elbow and begins staring at me — his face a frozen blank of pure white rage . . .

. . . so! . . . he's not coming clean after all . . . all he's doing is propping himself up on one elbow and staring at me . . . that's all! — that's it! . . . He doesn't have it in him because it's still the lie — the lie is still what matters . . . the lie is still what counts so he'll just keep staring at me like he's staring now . . . not blinking — not saying anything . . . and the disappointment . . . the unbearable heartbreaking disappointment of finally knowing who this person really is — of finally knowing who I married . . . "So tell me Mr. Columbus," I ask — "what is love?"

"My conscience is clear," he laughs as he looks away with cold rigid fury — "Now — Can we go to sleep?"

". . . sure," I answer, calm and contained as though I had gathered myself, like I were a huge white sheet that I finally folded into a small neat ball . . . "but tell me," I say as I look at my watch as I walk over to the window, pull back the curtain, and look out . . . "beside that heavy gardenia perfume that's all over you all the time — who calls here at all hours of the night and when I pick the receiver up . . . whoever it is hangs up?" I say as I watch a nervous blink begin, as well as a certain telltale twitch in his left shoulder that always happens when he gets nervous . . .

"and," I ask, still holding the curtain back so whoever it is out there can see me looking out . . . *Me — Instead of Him this time!* . . . "who drives through the alley every night in a dark red Jaguar convertible, flashes her headlights on and off, and then toots twice . . . like right now . . . Come over and have a look Mr. Columbus — Come on!" I say. "Come here and see for yourself if you don't believe me" . . . as a dark red Jaguar convertible goes slowly past the back of the building blinking its headlights on and off . . . as it toots two times.

"How should I know?" he says as he looks first at his watch and then at the window . . .

"You're *lying*!" I say.

"Everybody lies!" he answers as he looks back at his watch and then at the window again as his hands with those ten fat penis fingers begin trembling — his left shoulder jumping wildly in fierce little nervous spasms . . .

. . . and as I'm looking at his face . . . and then at his hands like aspen leaves trembling in the wind — then at his shoulder . . . and then out the window where the dark red Jaguar convertible is slowly turning the corner as it keeps flashing its headlights on and off . . . I know beyond a doubt that I'm right — he has someone . . . and I know it . . . and he knows I know it . . . and he knows I've known it for a long time too . . . and he knows too . . . that all he has to do is tell the truth . . . because knowing and yet not knowing is driving me insane.

part eight

lies

one

"I've been waiting for you," I whisper, my breath appearing like steam in the freezing early hours as I'm sitting on our terrace in Trixie's old mink coat . . . "*'our rendezvous' like García Lorca said . . . 'arm to arm on the rim of the well,'*" I smile — "because we both know this can't go on — you know that as well as I," I smile like the hypocrite I am . . . the liar . . . the snake . . . authenticity ha! — I never made much progress in that department even though that was all I ever wanted . . . even though I really tried . . . god knows I tried I'm thinking as I smile at her again —

"But first," I whisper . . . "before I offer you a cigarette — tell me . . . who are you — I mean, really . . . are you an apparition — a goddess, a vision — a ghost? . . . Are you flesh or are you madness? . . . I have to know," I say as I keep smiling warmly — "Are you real or aren't you?" I ask as she comes toward me out of the shadows near the living room door wearing that same white chiffon gown all right — I'm not surprised . . . with that one thick rhinestone strap across her other shoulder . . . her head cocked back and over to one side — her glorious red wavy hair tumbling past her shoulders . . . as she places her hands on her hips and smiles . . .

"Tell me," I whisper as I keep smiling at her like the lick I am — the phony . . . no honor — no honesty . . . just the same old kiss-ass liar lying my head off like the lying snake I am . . . even with her — what have I learned? — nothing! — not even with my husband's mistress whom I should smack . . . but no, instead I keep smiling at her as I'm whispering sweetly . . . "are you an illusion — a delusion? . . . something along those lines . . . or am I mad?" I ask . . . "Lately I've begun to wonder . . . The fact is," I say, "I'm not sure I know what's what anymore — I've become confused . . ."

. . . *I've been waiting for you too,* she says — *That's why I've come tonight — I'm here to tell you everything,* she says as she looks straight at me with flat blank sightless eyes like two dark points of heartbreak frozen on her face . . .

. . . *But I'm warning you,* she says — *you may be shocked by what I have to say* she says as she sits down at the little metal table next to me, takes one of my cigarettes, lights it, and then inhales as she's staring at me in that curious way that two women who love the same man eye each other, almost like they're not seeing who they're looking at . . . but instead . . . staring with fascination at the other like they're looking in awe at the beginning of all creation . . . "oh, don't worry," I laugh a dishonest hypocritical little chuckle — surprised on the one hand that she's stepping into my trap so easily . . . so willingly . . . and on the other — thrilled to my marrow that I'm going to get her this time . . . once and for all — *"please —"* I smile like the loathsome fake, the despicable fraud I am . . . "go ahead," . . . I whisper . . . *"Please!"*

. . . *Well,* she says as she keeps staring at me with

those dead blank eyes . . . *you could say that I'm the sorrow that sweeps across a Sunday afternoon — "I'm the blackness that's in everything and there is no greater truth"* . . .

. . . "yes," I whisper, "I'm not surprised . . . but that's not all you are — that's not the whole story is it? — who else are you? . . . go ahead, tell me . . . are you more — are you something else — someone else? — come on," I smile . . . "don't be shy" . . .

. . . *Okay,* she says . . . *I'm the one who can never find — will never find any consolation on my little dash across the sun, and not because there wasn't enough* she laughs as she keeps staring at me with those flat blank sightless eyes . . . *but because there was too much — much too much! — more than I could bear* she says as she suddenly leaps up — dashes out her cigarette on my terrace floor with the tip of that gorgeous white satin shoe . . . and then . . . as though swept by some grave magnificent force . . . some dark exquisite impulse . . . throws back her head, raises her arms, and begins stamping her feet as she turns up her open hands and begins clap clap clapping clapping clapping, clap clap clapping clapping as her heels begin bang bang banging banging banging banging . . . faster, faster — her rage — her best bile and her truth as she pulls up her skirt as her heels keep bang bang banging banging banging hammering hammering banging hammering bang bang banging banging hammering hammering . . . *You ask me who I am — I'm great streaks of scarlet blood across a milky sky . . . I'm the aching spirit of some melancholy demon who swallows babies whole . . . I'm the pain,* she says, *that has no explanation — the sorrow you can never shed — I'm that agonizing jolt when you first wake out of sleep* she says as her feet are going faster . . . faster . . . like little vicious hammers that exalt the blackness . . . honor the pain . . . *That's who I am — the broken dreams, the empty promises . . . the sobbing in a night that never ends* she shouts as she keeps clap clap clapping clapping clapping clapping, clap clap clapping clapping her hands above her head as her feet keep bang bang banging banging banging banging hammering hammering bang bang banging banging banging banging like mean little furious hammers that keep bang bang banging banging bang bang banging banging banging ferociously across my terrace floor as she tucks in her chin and drops her skirt as she starts clap clap clapping clapping clapping clap clap clapping clapping clapping clapping clapping clapping her hands above her head with a look on her face of strength and rage . . . *this!* — her great flamenco of hate and pride . . . *this!* — her great flamenco that tears the heart with shards of broken dreams — the ones that she could never reach — never have . . . the ones that slipped away like blackbirds in the night . . . her great flamenco — *this!* — the only thing that's worthy of her heartbreak and her truth as she's staring at the ground as her hands keep clap clap clapping clapping clapping clap clap clapping clapping clapping, clapping clapping clapping clap clap clapping clapping as her heels keep bang bang banging banging banging banging banging, pounding pounding hammering, pounding hammering hammering banging banging banging banging across my terrace floor as her hands keep clap clap clapping clapping clapping clapping . . . "come on — who else are you," I whisper . . . "are you someone else? — some secret person I think I know about — tell me," I whisper as I stand up . . . the tension mounting . . . *yes,* she shouts as her hands keep clap clap clapping clapping clapping clapping as her heels keep bang bang banging banging pounding hammering hammering, pounding pounding bang bang banging banging banging banging . . . *I'm the lie!* she shouts — *that every woman ever lied in bed — I'm the fake,* she shouts . . . *that every woman ever faked* as she tossed her head and swirled her hip and moaned and screamed *oh god — oh god . . . that's who I am — The fake! — the lie!* she's shouting, her back to me as her heels keep bang bang banging banging hammering hammering banging banging bang bang banging banging banging banging . . . as I sneak up behind her . . .

"So that's who you are — I see," I whisper . . . "That's sad — So sad," I whisper . . . that you had to lie because you never knew how great you were — you never had a clue and that's so sad . . . "so sad," I say as tears come to my eyes . . . honest tears, tears of deep regret . . . "that you had to fake so you could give him all the pleasure that you could . . . and sadder too that you had to keep on faking . . . and faking . . . and faking . . . and that's so sad — so sad — with nothing there for you . . . not ever . . . not even once except the disgrace that you could never measure up — the humiliation . . . so much secret shame . . . so much . . . and throw in too the heartbreak that he never saw that great and generous spirit that you carried so exquisitely — he never noticed — never dreamed how much you gave," I whisper . . . as I start moving quietly forward toward her . . . and then very carefully . . . very very slowly . . . I place my hands on her back, "too bad," I whisper as I slowly . . . very carefully begin pushing her . . . slowly . . . very slowly . . . toward the wall with the little rail on top . . .

"I'm so sorry," I whisper as I keep pushing her . . . slowly . . . slowly . . . "that he loved you for everything except that great and bursting heart of tears — for everything except the intrinsic truth that was so deep in you that you have to dance and shout and cry . . . yet he never heard — no one did and that's so sad, so sad," I say as I keep pushing her . . . gently . . . gently . . . very carefully . . . forward . . . very slowly . . .

"So sorry," I whisper with tears streaming down my face . . . "that he never knew how smart you were — how kind — how full of hope — he never had a clue and that's so sad — so sad," I'm whispering as I keep pushing her . . . slowly . . . very carefully . . . very gently . . . forward . . . forward . . . as her feet keep bang bang banging banging, hammering hammering banging hammering, pounding pounding pounding pounding . . . as her hands keep clap clap clapping clapping clapping clapping above her head as I'm pushing

her . . . slowly . . . very carefully . . . closer . . . closer . . .
forward . . . as she keeps clap clap clapping clapping
clapping, clap clap clapping clapping clapping clapping
as she shouts . . . *Yes — That's who I am — the lie that
every woman ever lied in bed — I'm the lie that made her hate
herself as she slowly became someone else — something else
only who knows who or what . . . maybe a famous movie star*
she's shouting, her arms above her head as her hands
keep clap clap clapping clapping clapping clap clap clap-
ping clapping clapping clapping clapping clapping her
wild exquisite mad flamenco . . . as I'm guiding her . . .
gently . . . gently . . . carefully . . . up on to the wall . . .
then over the little railing . . . tottering . . . tottering . . .
just on the ledge . . . tottering . . . tottering . . . then
looking down for a second into the dark black street
below . . .

. . . finally . . . my first real honest act . . . I'm so sorry
Rita I whisper as I give a push . . . but I never figured
how else to get rid of you . . . god knows I tried . . .

afterword

Solomon Columbus in his crisp blue cotton nightshirt and expensive blue leather bedroom slippers both from Brooks Brothers, no robe — hazy and half asleep as he's being escorted into the early-morning alley behind the building by the three policemen who were the first ones on the scene . . . the sun just coming up behind the park — her body, almost completely destroyed by the impact . . . clothed in a red flannel nightgown and an old mink coat — her red tangled hair spread across the pavement in the blood that she was lying in facedown — her dyed red wavy hair — all that was recognizable, all that could be called "intact" as her husband gazes at her . . . stunned . . . his memory . . . flashing . . . on and off . . . on and off . . . to another Saturday morning . . . another pool of blood . . . another event that was too enormous to even begin to understand . . . something he never really "got" because it was too "ungettable" . . . the worst part he told her then so long ago is that "then isn't then" he said, "then is now" and it keeps on being "now" because you just don't "get it" . . . maybe you never did . . . maybe you never will he told her then so long ago . . . the passion he had for her up in the attic then when they were both so young and it was so hot up there in all the dust and cobwebs that "then" just keeps on being a forever now . . . forever . . . when he loved her then so madly . . . so wildly . . . so insanely . . . that's why you never confess — that's what Uncle Jack always said — even if they catch you in the act you still say nothing Uncle Jack would laugh — You say they're crazy — You say they're seeing things — Remember that because if you love her certain things are better never said . . . that was Uncle Jack's philosophy and that's what he thought too — that's how he had seen it too . . . and what's more . . . even though he loved her probably more than she even loved herself . . . he didn't want to tell her certain things . . . he felt that certain things belonged to him — that they were his — not hers . . . not everything was hers which she never understood — that line in the sand that everyone's entitled to — their space — their privacy . . . that line that says "don't cross" . . . and anyhow . . . they meant nothing to him . . . nothing . . . all of them . . . whores — call girls — kickbacks from another time — a bad habit — that was all . . . toys — carcasses that had no meaning . . . she was the only one — she was his life . . . his love . . . she was the only one from the moment he laid eyes on her as he sits down in the street beside her . . . leans over her lifeless body . . . and when the policemen's backs are turned . . . snatches the diamond barrette shaped like a star from deep inside her thick red tangled hair . . . his mother's diamond barette that he found under his father's arm on that terrible morning when he ran down the stairs and saw him lying there . . . then saw her diamond barrette that he snatched and hid — young as he was and held on to and never told — not anyone — not ever . . . and then . . . the night that Jacob was born . . . gave it to her with tears streaming down his face because she was the one — the only one . . . she was his love — his life . . . it was her from the first moment he laid eyes on her when she was so young . . . so beautiful . . . that first moment when something happened between them that was irrevocable . . . that first moment when the earth heaved — didn't she know — couldn't she tell . . . she had to know that it was always only her . . . only her . . . his gasping sobs choking him . . . his thick dumb tears . . . as he begins stroking her terrible tangled matted sad red hair.